Endure

EVOLVE SERIES, BOOK 4

A NOVEL BY

S.E. HALL

S.E. Hall

Cover Model: Shelby Leah, my sweet girl

Cover Design: Sommer Stein of Perfect Pear Creative

Editor: Katherine Tate

Formatter: Brenda Wright

Thank you all!

This book is intended for mature audiences only.

Table of Contents

Dedication

"You should name the last book, if you ever write it, Endure. And can we please get a Nanabug character in there somewhere?"

Done and done, Mama. Done and done.

XO,

Stephie

Endure

Prologue

"I do," the sweet promise fights its way past her trembling lips, barely kept tears swimming in her big brown eyes.

"I do too," he immediately parrots, an adoring grin, belonging only to her, on his face.

And I might be the only one who caught it, but there was definitely a subtle drop in his shoulders, telling me he also just let out a silent sigh of relief.

Maybe that's the *real* reason they'd switched things up, the bride saying "I do" first—he was worried she'd change her mind at the last minute—and not the gentlemanly "ladies first" excuse we were given.

I'd get a kick out of his discomfort…if I didn't know exactly how he felt.

"Son." The preacher fails to hide his own amusement, much like the crowd, their subdued wave of laughter rolling over the ceremony. "It's not your turn yet."

"With all due respect, sir, now works for me just fine. If she does, I do too, whatever it is. That simple. Gonna kiss her now." He starts to make his move, leaning in to claim her tiny mouth, but he's stopped short by the hand on his shoulder.

"We're not quite to that part either. There's still the exchanging of rings and my pronouncement." The man in the robe blushes as he tries to slow the eager groom down. All the while, every woman looking on is now audibly oohing and aahing.

"Well hop to it, your holiness. I'm itching to kiss my wife!"

His enthusiasm is as humorous as it is recognizable. There's no feeling in the world comparable—the impatience to begin the rest of your life with that *one* person—the only woman in the world who turns you into a blundering fool, no matter who's watching. The need to touch her so great, you'll babble your way through an argument, *with a man of God*, no matter who's listening.

He loves her. Without reason or restriction.

Unashamedly.

And watching this poor, pitiful young man fumble his way through the rest of the necessities, a bittersweet calm falls over me.

She and this marriage are both going to be just fine. No, better than fine... flourishing.

She will now be his, and he hers... and so, another chapter begins.

Chapter 1

In Flight Entertainment

-Dane-

"You think you can keep the women distracted long enough for me to beat that lil' fucker's ass and drag him out of here?"

There's not a whole lot I wouldn't do for Sawyer Beckett. Except that. Not only *won't* I help him with this half-cocked, completely unnecessary plan, but I couldn't even if I wanted to. There isn't a big enough diversion tactic to be concocted that will keep our women, or everyone in the vicinity for that matter, including the many security guards, from noticing him wailing on someone in the middle of an airport. And I'm pretty sure it'd change the pre-recorded "Code Orange" protocol announcement that repeats overhead to… an entirely different color.

Beckett needs to practice what he preaches and "simmer down," at least until we get through this destination wedding. He messes this up for her in any way, and I'll kill him with my own two hands.

"What exactly is your problem with Ryder?" I ask him.

Sawyer snarls, rolling his neck and popping his knuckles. "Beady-eyed little bastard keeps looking at me all funny and shit."

No, he doesn't. But, in the interest of limiting my time and energy to a language Sawyer actually speaks, I taper my reply to pack the hardest punch.

"If *you* quit staring at *him*, then you won't know what the hell he is, or isn't, looking at. So, maybe stop obsessing over this new lil' crush of yours and go find Emmett? I'm sure she could use your help with something." I suggest and point in the direction the ladies wandered.

"*Crush.*" He snorts. "Get fucked, Kendrick."

When all else fails, call Sawyer's manhood into question—works every time.

"And how the hell are *you* possibly the cool and collected one right now?" he asks.

"I'm always the cool one." I grin, with not so much as an eyelid twitch, refusing to acknowledge the trickle of sweat gliding its way down the back of my neck. "And I get fucked, often and very well. But thanks for your concern. Come on." I stand. "I'll go with you."

Thankfully, Sawyer finds Emmett right away, and I'm able to offload the man-child into her custody. Can't feel too sorry for her, she signed up for that job willingly.

As entertaining as it is to watch Emmett use her feminine ploys to placate him—the spell she somehow weaves over him still shocks me every time—my Laney's not with her, so I leave them to continue the search for my own little vixen.

Doesn't take me long, I spot her perfect ass and golden hair flowing down her back in the next store I scan.

She knows I'm there before I speak, her back straightening and a slight shift in her stance; the tangible current in the air I feel every time she nears a shared phenomenon. "Baby," I approach her from behind and wrap my arms around her waist, sneaking my face through her mane to *my* spot—the crook of her neck. "Gonna be boarding time soon, you might wanna speed it up."

"It's a long flight. I need, *stuff*," she huffs. It's *not* a long flight, under three hours in fact, but I don't point it out.

Instead, I chuckle as I survey her mountainous pile at the register—magazines, candy, salty snacks, juice, pop, gum, two neck pillows and a romance novel. "I can see that. I think you've got it covered."

"Don't start with me, Caveman." She jabs her elbow backward, her signature move that I'm always ready for and easily dodge. "I'm nervous."

"Relax, everything's gonna be fine." I kiss her neck. "Let me pay for your haul, then it should be about time to head out."

She scoffs, dismissing my assurance. "Where are my parents? Please tell me you didn't just leave them roaming around the airport alone?"

Jeff and Trish are on our commercial flight today because Jeff Walker "doesn't need the fancy-schmancy charity" of a private plane. His words, not mine. And Laney and I are here because she insisted on flying with her parents.

We'd already be there if the man wasn't as stubborn as his daughter.

But I've learned to pick my battles, and this was not one I had a snowball's chance in hell of winning—thus, I'm keeping my cool, secretly praying we manage to arrive in Jamaica before Laney completely loses it... or Sawyer terrorizes the entire airport.

Good times.

"Hey." I lock both hands on her hips and spin her to face me. "First of all, your parents aren't senile. Nor, to my knowledge, are they gypsies. So I'm not real concerned about them wandering off into the unchartered regions... of the airport. And your mom's pill kicked in, so she's napping, in the chair right next to your dad. They're both fine. Now chill out and kiss me. Better make it good too."

"And why is that?" She cocks her head to the side, with her snarky question.

"To convince me you're sorry for being such a snippy wench today." I wink.

Her eyes narrow to slits as she tries to squirm from my hold. "Kiss this," she snaps, but I simply laugh and seize her, *my*, mouth, because her little snits do nothing but turn me on more. I twirl the Disney "D" necklace that she never takes off between my fingers as I tongue-whip her into calming down, and when she's lax in my arms and the checkout girl clears her throat, I pull back.

No longer challenging, her eyes are now lazy-lidded, more hazel than brown, (the green in them always pops out when she gets turned on) and her breathing's slowed. Mission accomplished, I pat her butt and pivot her in the direction of her parents, gently *suggesting* she go check on them for herself while I pay.

"'K," she mutters. "Love you, and I'm sorry. I'm just—"

"Nervous, I know baby. But I got it, *we* got it, okay?"

She nods and finally gives me a real smile, sauntering away.

Yes, I turn and watch the sway of her ass as she does so. Never gets old.

You know how it's really loud on a plane, that constant, distorted hum overhead while in flight? So that even when the person in say, 2A is talking to their neighbor in 2B, they have to raise their voice some or lean in to be heard?

Imagine then, if you will, the volume at which Sawyer Beckett would need to bellow from the last row of first class to ask me, the *actual* occupant of 2A, something.

"This is all your fault, Kendrick! Even this punk kid I'm gonna kill agrees with me! Don't ya Ryder? And don't think I didn't catch that his name sounds like RIDE HER!" Sawyer screams as though we're the only ones on the plane. I don't have to turn around to know Emmett's crimson face is ducked in mortification and everyone seated around him is currently wondering, terrified of the answer, if security checked him thoroughly enough for stashed weapons... since he's clearly displaying some insane tendencies.

And I'm unsure exactly what's "my fault"—not that I'm gonna yell back and ask. Laney sticks out her hand to stop the stewardess, who unfortunately for her unknowing self, chooses now to walk by. "Are you people still possibly serving the very large, lunatic back there alcohol?" Laney asks her pointedly.

The attendant offers a sheepish smile and shrugs. "No ma'am. The lady with him already slipped me a note forbidding it.

But I believe he may be coercing the frightened young man seated in front of him to order and then stealing the drinks from him."

"Okaaay," Laney drawls out. "Just a thought." She holds up a finger, then uses it to tap her chin in the most condescendingly "I have a polite suggestion" manner possible. "How 'bout we *also* stop serving him too? Sound like a plan?"

If you really tried, you just might be able to catch a drip of the sarcasm in her question.

"And the blond man across from him, also in on the conspiracy?" The stewardess asks, biting back a smile, and referring to Zach… who must just be enjoying the show, because there's no way Sawyer's bullying *him* into surrendering over his drinks unwillingly.

"Oh, for the love of—" Laney throws off her seatbelt and stands, nearly knocking the woman in uniform over as she starts to stomp down the center aisle.

"Ma'am, the fasten seatbelt light is on!" The now alarmed attendant calls after her.

Laney stops dead in her tracks, pivots and glares at the poor woman. "Seems we're all making bad decisions today. I'll take my chances." And she's off again.

I let her go because A. I agree, they're out of control back there in what they're quickly turning into the hoodlum section and Emmett just doesn't possess that certain something it takes to settle them down when they're really on a roll, and B. they're a helluva lot more scared of Laney than they are of me.

I lay my head back against the headrest and close my eyes, recalling the last time Laney truly schooled Sawyer Beckett. Sure, they swap verbal jabs as though it's Olympic sport each and every time they converse, but sometimes, it's especially entertaining. It's been awhile since such epic an incident as what's about to happen has, but the memory of one of my very favorite episodes is as vivid as the day it occurred.

"*Hand Presley to me right now, Sawyer. You're gonna shake her brain loose! She's a baby, not a Magic Eight Ball!*"

"*I know how to soothe my own daughter, woman!*"

"*Obviously! She's crying harder now than when we walked in! If you flipped her over, a little triangle would pop up on her butt that says 'doesn't look good, try again later.' Dane, tell him Presley needs her Aunt Gidget!*"

"*Daney, please locate your ballsack, if it's even still there, and remind your boss lady here that I don't take well to her critiquing my parenting!*"

"*That's it, I'm calling Emmett!*" Laney didn't even get her phone out of her pocket before Sawyer was complying.

"*Do. Not. Call. Emmy.*" Sawyer handed over Presley, Laney's favorite lil' person in the whole world, then, and the baby was fast asleep on her shoulder within seconds.

"*See,*" Laney whispered roughly. "*You'd be a lot better off if you'd start listening right when I start speaking, Saw. I'm Presley's favorite, everyone knows that. But make sure to tell Whitley about this, just in case she's forgotten.*"

"*Fuck, you're—*"

"*Sawyer!*" Laney scorned in a muted hiss, covering Presley's ear with one hand. "*You spell out F-U-C-K or say nothing at all! I'll not have my niece growing up with a trash mouth like yours! Now quit talking or you'll wake her up. Not to mention ruin her chances of getting into any pre-school not run by sailors!*"

"How about 'F bomb'?"' he suggested, his expression that of sincere belief he'd just hatched and proposed a brilliant alternative.

"Bombs? You want to mention bombs to the baby? Great idea, and then let's make sure we cover guns, gangs and the Illuminati!" Laney rolled her eyes and shook her head in exasperated disbelief. "Please tell me you're not in charge of bedtime stories. Dane, I'm serious, do something."

I did nothing; but stand back and watch, trying not to laugh so loud as to wake up Presley.

God, I love my Laney.

The very woman returns to her seat beside me just as the memory fades, dropping down with an annoyed huff.

"You get 'em lined out, boss?" I ask, chuckle tamed.

"Yeah, I cut them off. I don't know what's gotten into them today. Like *they* should be the ones who're antsy."

"They're not antsy, they're headed to paradise, a vacation for all of them. Just getting started early." I explain.

"Well, with any luck, they'll pass out from their early start as soon as we land."

"Baby," I now laugh freely. "There's nothing strong enough on this plane to put them on their asses. Takes more than a few hours and all the alcohol on board to lay out men of their size."

"Shoulda slipped 'em a Mickey," she grumbles, crossing her arms.

"You don't even know what that means, gangsta. Why don't you read that book you bought? You set them straight, so they won't get any worse."

"Okay." She sighs, her shoulders relaxing marginally. "How much longer till we're there?"

"Don't ask, just read your book."

Chapter 2

Crew Control

-Laney-

This is not our first trip, or wedding, as a group, so why *certain people* are acting like it's the first time we've let them out of their cages, I'm not quite sure. A blind man could see I'm already on edge… they know better than to test me.

But this is my *Crew*. A crazy, crude conglomeration of people that are more than just my friends; they're my family— *we're a family*. The ones who can make each other laugh or cry the hardest, the people who you never have to question whether or not you can count on them.

Over the years, we've lost, and gained, some members. Some by choice, others by fate. Life has tried several times to splinter our foundation, topple our fortress—and failed. Our faith; in God, ourselves, and each other has been tested beyond measure, multiple times… but in the end, the crew saves the ship— Every. Single. Time. And we make it through the storm.

Our vessel may have cracks and dings, tatters in its sail, and sometimes takes on water… but it still cuts through the waves with authority.

Unsinkable.

The overwhelming amount of loyalty and camaraderie that, occasionally, comes along with bouts of mayhem and disorderly conduct, is more than worth it. Reminding myself of this is the only thing stopping me short of slapping some sense into the yahoos back there—needing my foot up their asses as badly as I need a Xanax.

"Slugger," my dad—who still calls me Slugger, and I still love it—leans forward to speak to me from across the aisle, no more fooled into thinking I'm actually reading this damn book as he is that I'm over here silently contemplating Astrophysics. "You talk to Brynn about what I said?"

Make that two Xanax, STAT.

"No, Dad." I turn my head away from him to roll my eyes, just in time to catch Dane make a half-ass attempt to cover his smirk.

Only *my* father would somehow mistake now as a good time to discuss, and by discuss I mean his giving a full-on critique, of one of my pitchers.

There's not a thing wrong with *any* of my pitchers, least of all Brynn. She's an amazing athlete, with a natural, God-given talent that's truly an honor to watch, and my father knows it. He's just… well, he's just how he is about softball. Never gonna change. Works for me—wouldn't have him any other way.

Except now, on the flight from hell, when I'm already feeling postal… and certainly not in the mood to dissect Brynn's technique.

"The ball's coming out before her foot's down." *Maybe once every twentieth pitch; heaven forbid she's not perfect.* "You'd think she'd have learned to plant and peel in 10U," my dad shakes his head and clucks his tongue. "Guess not. Some of my coaching could've stopped that problem a long time ago."

When I don't immediately answer him, he leans back his chair, giving me a chance to jerk my head to Dane. "Hello? Feel free to jump in here anytime!"

"Correct your father on *softball?* Um, pass," he winks and kisses the end of my nose. "Your dad, your team, your sport."

Damn right it's my team.

After graduating from Georgia Southern, with my degree in Kinesiology, minor in History, I was asked to stay on as one of the assistant softball coaches. So I did. And worked the young women who graced the diamond into finely-tuned machines, while waiting… until I was the head coach.

"Perhaps Brynn's *problem* is the gray-haired communist barking at her from the fence on every pitch?" I suggest in a low growl.

"Maybe." Dane chuckles. "You should tell him that. Lemme know how that works out for ya."

"Fine. Sit there all silent then, but you're not getting laid this entire trip." I quirk a brow as I hiss out the kill shot.

He leans into me, his warm breath bathing my ear, and rubs my leg slowly, climbing closer to the apex of my thighs with each glide. "You and I both know that's not true, baby. Need me to prove it? I'd be more than happy to keep talking, get those legs of yours rubbing together even faster, that sweet ass squirming in your seat, right in front of your father. Is that what you need?" He murmurs, in a low, raspy taunt, his lips hinting to touch my heating skin. "If you think you can hide your reaction, I'm positive I can hide what my fingers are doing to you. Wanna give it a try?"

"I hate you sometimes," I seethe, forcing my thighs and ass to remain as still as possible and the building desire out of my voice.

"But you love what only I can do to your body *all* the time. Now turn around and finish your conversation, *if* you're not too worked up to concentrate that is. Oh, and look." He peers over my shoulder. "Your mom's awake. Should be a real party now."

I glance back and sure enough, Mom's up and at 'em, bright eyed and bushy tailed. My parents are now… hmmm, best friends? Company for each other? Not sure, and I don't need a label for it, I'm just thrilled they get along so well and I can invite them both to things.

There're still some days Mom doesn't know who is who, but they're fewer and farther between since Dane got her the best doctor to be found. I thank God, and Dane, every day that I have her back in my life, to stay. Pretty sure my Dad does too—especially since his dating Rosemary ceased a long time ago. Fine by me. Sure, Rosemary was nice enough, but she had this *one hair* sticking out of this *one mole* on her chin… I mean seriously, how do you *not* see it? Everyone else does! Grab the tweezers, one good yank, done! Drove me insane.

Everyone should have at least one person in their life with the balls to tell them, "no ma'am, that's just not okay." A friend who sees the booger in your nose, or knows damn good and well that the pants you're wearing were too tight five years ago and says nothing?

No friend at all.

Anyway, I digress.

"Morning, Mom," I chirp, giddy and gearing up for the tag team I have planned that my dad will never see coming. *Another benefit of my parents being together so much—the "two against one" strategy I often employ.* "I'm glad you're awake. Daddy here was just telling me all the things wrong with Brynn's pitching. Any thoughts on the matter?" I ask, infused with an almost choking amount of innocence.

"Pure evil," Dane mumbles in my ear, and receives a friendly reminder that he bowed out of this conversation, in the form of an elbow to his ribs. *Didn't dodge that one now did he?*

"Jefferson Walker!" My mother swallows the whole lure I cast in one gulp, screeching at a volume that exceeds my expectations. "What exactly is it that you have to say? I'm awake and listening now, so *please*, do fill me in."

"Trish." My dad stink eyes me then runs a hand down his face. "You know absolutely nothing about pitching, and I made one comment. *Your daughter* just can't take the slightest criticism."

Bull's-eye! When mom's lucid, she's razor sharp, and Daddy secretly loves the interaction. So, that oughta keep my parents occupied for a while. I smile to myself and pull out my notebook; time to capitalize on this new adrenaline rush and work on my upcoming speech.

I'm more than positive Whitley has some spotlight stealer of her own planned, highly likely in the form of song (insert eye roll) and I refuse to be outdone.

Love Whitley to death, and she may know more than me about super important stuff such as which fork to use when or the life-threatening hazards of wearing black and brown at the same time, but words? The right ones, at the right time, in the right way?

That's all me.

"At this time, we ask that you please turn off all electronic devices, make sure any items are securely stowed under the seat in front of you and that your seatbelt's fastened as we begin our initial descent into Jamaica. The local time is 4 p.m. with a current temperature of 82 degrees. Thank you for flying with us today and enjoy your stay."

This is it. One step closer to the life changing event.

"You ready for this?" Dane asks me with a confident tilt of his lush lips, silently telling me, as always—everything will be all right.

And anything that's not; he'll fix.

"Yeah," I find his hand and squeeze, feigning a grin in hopes of reassuring him, which he'll no doubt see right through. "I'm good."

Even if I'm not, he is.

Where I fall short, he'll carry me. So whether or not I'm actually ready doesn't matter, because Dane Kendrick will always pick up where I leave off. And in that, I draw a strength not entirely my own.

Chapter 3

Nowhere to Hide

-Dane-

Just a fact, and quite possibly a recurring nightmare for any outsider to have witnessed an occurrence, any "crew" activity is an automatic guarantee for some sort of spectacle—often before it's even totally underway. Which is why, I'd be shocked if Whitley *wasn't* outside, squawking and wildly flapping her arms, trying to get past the armed customs guards. So much for waiting *inside* the airport. Or the enforcement of FAA rules, of which I'm positive she's violating at least three.

Somewhat hidden behind the fan of her blond hair, blowing out in all directions with her rigorous attempts at subterfuge, stands Evan, the most patient, easy-going man I've ever known. Calm, hands in his pockets, immune to Whitley's spastic behavior, he simply watches on and laughs. Along with Bennett, also seemingly unfazed by the very real possibility Whitley may be shot and/or locked up in a Jamaican holding cell at any point.

"I'd spank your ass if you tried that," I growl in Laney's ear, wrapping my arm tighter around her waist.

"I'm aware," she deadpans, and I know without looking, rolls her eyes.

Guess the guards are in a good mood today, or know the difference between a threatening crazy and just plain crazy because Whitley's waiting, unshackled, for us when we make it through the line.

"You made it! Yay!" Whitley shrills, throwing her arms around Laney. "Where's everyone else?"

"If by everyone else you mean Shitfaced, Instigator and poor Emmett, they were all several rows behind us, should be coming along any minute. Sobered up, I hope." Laney grimaces. "Zach was at two sheets, Sawyer borderline unconscious, Ryder scared to breathe and Emmett... probably still contemplating suicide."

And one thinks Whitley exaggerates? I say nothing, biting back my laugh.

"Oh no, they don't." Whitley's brow crinkles and both hands fly to her hips. "I simply won't tolerate it."

Here we go.

"Dane, grab Trish's bag please," Mr. Walker says to me and I rush to help, leaving the girls to plan their counter-attack.

"So handsome." Laney's mom pats my cheek, like she always does. "Why, if I weren't old enough to be your mother and—"

"Trisha," Mr. Walker interrupts her in grave disapproval and saves me the familiar, but no less embarrassing, admiration. "Keep walking, dear, it's hot out here."

Finally *inside* the actual airport, Evan and Bennett join the rest of our group, no longer just hangin' out as if in no one else's way, each giving Laney and her parents hugs.

"Where's Zach and Saw? Lemme guess, they've been detained for questioning, regarding some *incident*, I won't even wager a guess on, during the flight?" Evan laughs while shaking my hand.

I'm about to tell him how scarily close to the truth he actually is, when Sawyer's voice booms out. "We're right here, you twig packin' mother—"

"Sawyer! My parents, much?" Laney scolds him, loudly, "Help your wife with her bag before I kick your ass and do it myself!"

"Come on, Emmy." Sawyer's voice and expression immediately soften as he turns to his Achilles', one of only two people he'll literally morph before your eyes for—his wife. The other, his daughter Presley.

"You wound me, man," Zach claps Evan on the shoulder. "Even if I'd been held up, it'd only be to cover Sawyer's back. You know I never cause trouble."

"Oh, please," Laney scoffs. "Emmett, you sat with them, help me out here."

"Tempting." Emmett grins. "But looks like we're ready to go."

And we are, Ryder having arrived, leery and standing as far back as possible without actually exiting the airport. But

Whitley wastes no time hugging and including him. "Okay, that's everyone this round! We've got a van waiting out front, let's load up. Wait until you see the resort, it's amazing! You did well, Dane."

I couldn't be more down with that plan, ready for things to be "less crowded," a.k.a alone with Laney.

"You go ahead with your folks to the van and make those phone calls I know are killing ya. I'll grab the rest of our luggage." I kiss Laney's cheek and she readily agrees.

"I'll help ya," Evan offers, Zach and Sawyer nodding in agreement. So the men head toward baggage claim, the women, parents and Ryder, to the van.

"So, you boys ready for this?" Zach asks, antagonistic lilt to his voice and spring in his step.

"As I'll ever be." Evan groans. "Makes for a long trip when Whit insists on arriving so much earlier than everyone else."

"Sucks to be you, man. But it's damn good to be me. I'm gonna sit back in the pool, let them bring me my drinks and find some nice, exotic beauty who nods and shoves her tits further against me with every word I say." Zach laughs.

"No shit? What happened to that one chick, Donna, was it?" Sawyer asks. "She was hot."

"It is Donna, and she's still hot. I'll see her when I get back, but we're not committed or anything. Not even close."

Because Zach doesn't do commitments, I don't add aloud. Zach Reece is the nicest guy you'll ever meet, level-headed, honest, successful... but burned one too many times, never really fully rising from the ashes. Found out his high-school sweetheart was cheating via Facebook, a girl he invested all his most vulnerable, developmental years in, and I suspect, genuinely loved. Then he *saw* Avery cheat on him, a raunchy display, in the middle of the K, humiliated and deceived once again. And the real doozy? Some random biker-chick threesome we never really got the whole story on—but he spent a while stewing over that one—debating whether to go track her down or sleep with a loaded gun and one eye open.

Can't say I really blame him for his commitment phobia and faithlessness in faith. He seems happy enough now though, coaching football at a junior high where he also teaches Algebra, owns his own home and motorcycle, and has a gorgeous date for every gathering. Except this one.

"Ya'll gotta come up with a golf game or something for just the guys," Evan begs. "Whitley's driving me crazy with all this wedding planning stuff. Hummingbird's not so cute when she's on event coordinating crack."

"Um, I paid for the all-inclusive package. The wedding is planned," I interject, confused.

"You should ask for a refund," Evan laughs. "Better yet, don't say anything, cause they might demand *more* money, hazard pay. Whitley's been bugging the crap out of them."

I honestly... don't know what to say to that.

Zach and Sawyer laugh at our expense as we grab our suitcases off the turn belt and head out to the van.

"Okay, so everyone get checked and changed or whatever, then we'll all meet at the pool, in say, an hour?" Whitley, self-deemed social director, who's obviously taken to freebasing Adderall, claps her hands when we reach our ride.

"Or—" I step forward. "Laney and I will find you all later, after we're *rested*."

"Dane." Laney pretends to disagree in a low hum, but with one glance her way, and her hand already gliding down my back to land on my ass, she loses her protest.

"Seriously? It was only a three hour flight! Surely you can, um, wait to—"

"Whit." Evan chuckles, cutting off his wife's stammering protest with an arm around her shoulder and kiss to her head. "Let's head to the resort, get some food in you, and play it by ear. When's the last time you down shifted to eat?"

And just when I think Evan's squashed further announcement in front of Mr. Walker that I'm about to ravage his daughter... Sawyer chimes in.

"I like Kendrick's plan. Everyone load your asses in! Emmy, you can help me sweat out some of this alcohol when we get there woman." He all but pushes her in as she offers everyone an apologetic smile over her shoulder.

Yeah, not an awkward ride at all... luckily, the resort's only about twenty minutes away.

And Whitley, doesn't quit yammering the entire time, saving the rest of us any effort at filler conversation.

"Well then," Mr. Walker clears his throat and shrinks me with a pointed scowl when we're unloaded. Seriously, if the furrow in his brows were any deeper, they'd declare it a landmark and name it after a dead president. "Trish and I will need to get settled in too, perhaps catch a nap. I'm sure we'll see everyone later."

Sawyer dragged Em away almost before the van even came to a full stop, so after Laney's parents depart and Evan persuades Whitley to go eat that leaves me, Laney, Zach and Bennett. No idea where Ryder disappeared to.

"Come on, Ben. Let's find some fun." Zach takes her hand and with a timid look back over her shoulder at me, *strange*, she accepts and lets him lead her away.

"You ready to go see where we're staying?" I sidle up, flush against Laney's body and seek out her neck, her sweet, signature scent of lavender calling to my baser desires.

Her soft sigh is my answer.

Bags delivered, bellboy paid… I've waited long enough for her to anxiously tinker about the room in silence. You've seen one vacation suite, you've seen 'em all, and nothing here warrants her prolonged, pseudo fascination. I'll never understand the vast range of emotions swirling through her right now. There's a lot about to happen, it's affecting me too, but obviously, not to the same degree. Laney is, in fact, and to my delight, a woman… so yeah, we don't think the same way. But one thing I understand better than anyone, even my gorgeous Disney herself, is how to steer her mind elsewhere.

"Come here." I beckon her with respectful, but unyielding, emphasis as I kick off my shoes and socks.

"Huh?" She stalls with a transparent whisper over her shoulder.

"Come to me, Laney." I unbutton my shirt, but leave it on, for her to remove how she sees fit. The warning peel of my zipper echoes through the room and her shoulders draw up in anticipation, a muted gasp ghosting past her lips.

Stubborn, she remains at the window, back to me as she stares out at the tropical scenery I suspect she wishes to escape to, searching for answers to questions unvoiced, worries trying to steal her away from me.

It won't be allowed.

And she knows it.

Laney is mine; my love, my life, my solace... and I don't share. With anything, even things unseen. If she's not "here" with me, then I have two choices: join her wherever it is she's gone, or bring her back. And because I know her better than I know myself, I don't have to wonder which option is the right one. She *wants* to be in the now for this momentous trip, occasion. She *needs* me to overpower anything encumbering that.

My girl sets the most thrilling of traps. Wordlessly depending on me to walk right into them—which I will continue to do as long as I have legs and life with which to walk.

I destroy the gap between us, pressing my body to her back, hands kneading her shoulders. "Whose baby are you?" I ask upon the satiny skin where her neck and shoulder merge, specifically for my mouth. "Tell me."

"Yours." She expels her nerves in a ragged exhale, letting her weight collapse back against me. "Always yours."

"Turn around and make me believe it," I demand in calm absoluteness.

No one else ever saw it, caught on, *and no one ever will, now;* my intuitive discovery, our secret... but Laney is a *very* strong-willed woman, who only bends to the will of a man with equal or more strength, enough so to coerce, *seduce*, out the soft, sweet girl inside her. And the foresight to recognize when such force will be welcomed versus when she'll strike in protest like a viper.

That ever grateful man is me.

"Dane." She spins, a tinge of annoyance in her tone. "We don't have time for this. I'm fine, let's—"

"Fuck until you're a recognizable version of *my* Laney again? Good idea, baby." I wink and grip her ass, hard, in both hands. "Up," I insist, catching her as she instantly, instinctually, complies. "Legs around me," my voice now huskier as I carry her toward the bed, her already hot center warming me through my jeans.

At the edge of the California King, I set her on her feet. "Want you naked. Slow and sassy, take your time. But eyes on me. Think only of me; what you're giving me, to take. Any. Way. I. Want."

The rise and fall of her chest triples in time, a wanting flush creeping up her neck as that little tongue pokes out to wet both lips.

"You want it, don't you?" I rub myself through my pants, eyes fixed on her own laden pair. She nods, unbuttoning her shirt with a taunting lack of urgency. "How bad? Tell me."

"Very," she breathes out. "I need you, Dane." She shrugs off her top and tosses it aside, cupping her breasts through the sheer lace.

"Lay down," I growl, out of patience.

Chapter 4

Conquered by the Caveman

-Laney-

Staring up at him from my position flat on my back (of course I listened to his growly demand), my man of few words speaks volumes as he towers over me, causing my breathing to hasten. His amber eyes smolder, pupils so dilated the black threatens to overtake the brown, and a small tick triggers in the tense line of his jaw. He's in hunter mode and I'm his prey, quivering from the inside out, waiting for him to pounce.

"I don't like it when you leave me. Have I ever let you shut me out?" He arches a dark brow in rhetorical challenge, yet I still shake my head. "That hasn't changed," he grunts, curling his fingers around my ankles and tugging me forward till I'm all but hanging off the bed. "I think my baby," he lifts one of my legs, kissing up the inside of my calf, "needs reminded," higher still, "that it's my job, my pleasure, to take care of her."

"I'm right here," I manage to eke out breathlessly.

"No, you're not. But you will be." His simple statement's filled with a confidence he's more than earned, time and time again, and of course, joined by a saucy wink that makes me melt. Every. Single. Time.

There was a time that I'd have laughed in the face of anyone who even thought about suggesting that I'd one day go weak-kneed and pliant under a man's upper-handedness.

Now I'd laugh at myself, a true fool, if I so much as debated, for as little as a split second, of attempting to resist the patented brand of bossy that only Dane Kendrick can deal out.

And bending, literally and figuratively, to his will? It never feels like "caving" or "giving in"… it feels like reflex. Natural.

I *want* to make him happy, as happy as he makes me. And in *no* way do I ever want to discourage his domineering ways. Sure, sometimes he makes things more difficult than they have to be, but more often than not, those ways of his make me feel safe and cherished. And I *definitely* don't want to complain in the daylight only to have him misunderstand and dial it down in the bedroom.

His large, but nimble, hands make easy work of unfastening my pants and latching onto both the denim and lace waistbands. "Lift," he demands and bares me from the waist down with one quick tug. The way his gaze bores into me, it's so penetrative that it feels like a physical touch. And the tongue I know to be unworldly talented gliding over his bottom lip, has me panting, dying for him to glide it over me instead. A bullet of greedy need zings through me, before he's even begun the really wicked things I know are coming, that virile, potent command of his I ache for.

I watch with growing hunger as he sheds his shirt, revealing his beautiful torso; tan, taut shoulders, a light smattering of dark hair on his chest, fine lines tapering down to an abdomen so defined and lickable, it should be illegal. I will *never* tire of Dane's body, a thing of true beauty that he "owns" with humble arrogance. My own private playground.

He may think *he's* the king of territorialism, but that sculpted, mouthwatering physique he's workin' with belongs. To. Me. And I can have it any time I want, because that package (yeah, that one too), comes with an insatiable appetite that craves me just as much as I crave him.

My unsteady breathing grows louder than I can control and he leers down at me, silently telling me with the cocky glimmer in his eyes that he knows exactly what he's doing to me. "Now she's coming around," he taunts in sly pride as he pushes his pants and black boxer briefs over his hips and down to the floor. "You want me, baby?"

I nod, scooting back like a horny lil' crab and position myself lengthwise on the bed to give him plenty of room to conquer me.

He joins me on the bed in a predatory crawl, hovering over me now, and rids me of my bra in a dizzying flurry of precision. "I didn't quite hear you." His breath fans over my face as he runs his nose along the length of mine. "Was that a yes?"

Certain things, Dane *has* to hear me actually say.

So much so, he'll hold back with infuriating self-control until he goads the words from me. Sometimes I'm simply too delirious with want to answer, but often, I deny him on purpose—because he gets unthinkably harder and more aggressive with every affirmation I do finally give aloud. And when I give in and he unleashes all that pent-up deprivation on me, it's ungodly euphoric.

"Say it, baby. Tell me how bad you want it," his voice strained and authoritative.

Oh, yeah, there's the voraciousness in his eyes. He's ready.

"You know I want you, always. I love you, Dane." I reach up to run one hand through his thick, brown hair, and wrap the other around his neck, pulling his mouth down to mine.

He groans into our kiss, using his hips wedged between my legs to push them farther apart. His hard length jerks between us and seeks out my core where he slides through my wetness, pressing down harder with each pass over my clit, prodding just a hint deeper with every swipe near my entrance. The veins and head are now so engorged, I can feel them bump along me deliciously.

"Dane," I moan, sucking on his bottom lip, digging my fingers into the slickening skin of his neck. "Love me. Now."

He lifts off me, pushing my knees up to meet my chest then leans forward again to pin them there with his weight. No wiggle room allowed. Using only one of his hands to trap both of mine over my head roughly, the other begins its slow tease. One fingertip circles around first the left, then the right nipple of my heaving breasts, his smile devilish as the peaks harden and seem to reach up and out for him.

"I know my Disney," he growls. "Her mind, soul, and especially," he aligns with my wet and oh-so-ready center, "her body. You're gonna take it all for me at once, aren't ya baby? You want my cock deep and fast?"

"God, yes," I moan.

With a long, hoarse exhale, he shoves all the way inside me, invading me physically and emotionally. It's rough, but beautiful. He murmurs his approval as a soft whimper escapes me, and instantly, every single thing or thought that isn't "us" disappears. My mind is now void of all but the feel of his rigid width thrusting in and out of me, his firm grip on my wrists and his warm mouth sucking my breasts, across my collarbone and up my neck.

"I've got you," he assures in my ear, low and raspy. "Always. Anything. I've," thrust, "got," a torturous rotation of his hips, swirling his length inside me to stroke adoration along each and every spot, "you. Squeeze around my dick baby. You know how I like it."

I love his vulgar mouth, I could probably come from his words alone.

I flex my inner muscles, constrict and release, over and over, fighting my lids that want to close in ecstasy to take in the sight of him loving me. Looking up at him, like this, his head back, mouth open, an endless grumble working its way up from deep within his chest... it's my favorite view in the whole world. A light sheen of exertion glitters on his skin, the heady scent of Dane and male desire fogging my brain. "Fuck yes baby, just like that. So damn good, hot, and *mine*," he roars, dropping his sweat coated body back down to hood mine. His chest hairs abrade my nipples deliciously and his pelvis now flush, rubs my clit with each plunge inside me, begging for my climax.

"Dane, oh, *please*." I buck and writhe beneath him, never able to get close enough, and fight his hold on my wrists. He releases them and my hands fly to his shoulders where I cling for leverage, craving the full impact of his drives inside me. "Harder, harder, babe. I need it."

The headboard bangs against the wall as he slams into me with abandon, burying his face in my neck, licking the sweat from my skin. "Laney, God, I love you." He sneaks his thumb between us with no falter in his rhythm or force, working my clit expertly. "Come baby, wanna feel your sweet pussy beg for it. Damn close, finish me Laney."

So dirty he talks—but I can always also hear the purity—only for me, in our time alone, he sends me soaring. With a single, endless keen, I contract around him, but at the same time relax; the contradictive, euphoric combination of exploding for the love of my life. He fills me with thick, wet warmth in several short, shallow thrusts, then collapses half on top, half to the side of me, and nuzzles his face in the crook of my neck once more.

It's been his "go to" spot for as long as I can remember.

Once he's caught his breath, he murmurs with a kiss to my neck, "Anything you wanna talk about?"

I snicker and pull him closer against me. "Not a thing, Caveman. All better now."

After our shared, long and gluttonous shower, we continue taking our time getting ready to go spend time with everyone else. Although, I must admit, I could use the replenishment of a nice dinner. Between my wandering mind, which Dane insisted wander its way right back to him, and the nervous exhilaration of upcoming events… my always insatiable Caveman was feeling extra barbaric on round two.

As if on cue, both our phones chime with an incoming message. That can only mean one thing, group text, hated by more of the Crew than not. I'd wager an internal organ, Whitley is the creator of said text-bomb, whose man loathes this particular form of communication beyond measure.

Sure enough. One glance at my phone and it's confirmed, my kidneys are safe.

Whitley: I've got our table reserved in the restaurant downstairs for 7 p.m. That's one hour, people! Plenty of time to finish up any "resting."

Evan: For God's sake, woman! I'm standing right beside you. Why am I on this group text? And why am I still... never mind.

Gotta love Whitley. She never ceases to provide endless entertainment by ruffling Evan's feathers, for us to watch and enjoy.

That shit's funny.

Zach: Me & Ben are ready. See ya down there.

"Dane, will you—" I stall when I turn and find him on the phone in the room, already talking to one of my parents, before I could even finish asking him to do just that.

The simplest of tasks, those little random acts of synchrony that serve as reminders that another soul shares space with your own... mean the most.

My phone vibrates in my hand, startling me from my whimsical musings, and I glance back down the screen.

Sawyer: Me & Em are already down here. She's shitfaced, dancing on the bar and causing a scene, so hurry up all you slow fuckers. She's out of control.

Oh, Sawyer, I roll my eyes. Emmett is doing no such thing, and how he never fails to come up with this stuff, remains a mystery. I can only imagine it might get nerve-wracking for sweet Emmett sometimes, but I'm also pretty positive it keeps life spontaneous and interesting. And that counts for so many somethings.

I'm two thumbs ready to text our RSVP when Dane hangs up the phone. "Your parents already ordered room service and wanna sit this one out. Guess the busy day, flight and all, wiped 'em out."

"Are they okay? Do I need to go check on them?"

He chuckles lightly and shakes his head. "Your dad knew you'd say that. He made me promise to tell you." He deepens his voice and does his best Jeff Walker impersonation. "We're just a little old, a little tired, Slugger. You go on and have yourself a good time, without worrying."

"And you—"

"Yes." He regains his normal voice and simpers, a warm smile tugging at the corner of his mouth. "I believe him."

"Well, okay then." I shrug and take him at his word, always do, and return my attention to my phone.

Me: We'll be down in a sec. My parents are sitting out this round.

Whitley: It's a date! (insert several of those little party popper emojis)

Evan: Great, all settled then. This message is now dead. Everyone delete it and feel free to text mono e mono amongst yourselves going forward.

Sawyer: RT Evan.

Sawyer: My bad, deleting for real now.

Dane exhales through his nose and runs a hand back through his hair, which somehow always makes it look like he styled it all sexy that way on purpose. With a dash of humor in it, he sighs. "Gonna be a long trip."

He's absolutely right, but I know for certain he's also more than aware we have the best group of friends one could ever dare hope for. I wouldn't change a single thing about a single one of them... and neither would he.

We make our way down to the restaurant, hand in hand, to find nothing that surprises me.

Whitley's standing up, waving her arms wildly as though I'm not staring straight at her and might somehow miss them. Sawyer's indicating another round for the table to the passing waiter, and not a bit surprising, Emmett is seated beside him, *not* on the bar and/or seemingly out of control. Zach has one arm slung over the back of Bennett's chair, body turned into her as she tosses her head back and giggles at something he's just said.

The whole "too close for comfort" thing comes to mind for a split second, but dismiss even faster because the special, irreplaceable closeness of the Crew *is* comfort, definitively. Who am I to put parameters on that security?

You know the saying "lightning never strikes twice?" I'm not sure how it ever became a saying, because it's grossly inaccurate.

In fact, there's a ton of places that have been struck *more* than twice in a single storm! (Yes, I looked it up.) For example, on the night of February 5, 2008, a radio tower in Lexington, Kentucky was struck eleven times within twenty minutes.

Hold on to that little gem; it'll be on Jeopardy one day and you'll wow all your friends by knowing the answer, *in the form of a question of course.*

I have a mental list of factoids like that, because, well, it was one of the ways I tried to help Dane make sense of things when we lost Tate.

After the car wreck that almost killed Tate during my freshman year of college, Dane had a lot of trouble processing the sick twist of fate that his brother had survived one near-fatal crash...only to turn around and *not* survive another one a few years later. He kept saying *"what are the odds,"* over and over... so I looked up the odds; on the literal, two time wreck victims, and the metaphorical, lightning strikes. It did seem to help, a little.

Two of the most important people in my life, had lost one of the most important in theirs. Of course I still worry about Dane, especially on special dates, holidays... but Dane isn't alone... like Bennett.

And with the reminding ache in my chest, I move to her side, leaning down to wrap her in an unexpected hug.

"What was that for?" she smiles up at me and asks, cheeks beautifully flushed from the half-empty glass of wine she sets down.

I shrug, with a loving grin of my own. "Just because. Do I need a reason?"

"Nope. Never. Have a seat, sista." She pats the empty chair beside her and I take it, Dane sliding in to the spot on my left.

Chapter 5

How Many in Your Party?

-Dane-

Dinner is… dinner, I suppose. Sawyer's being Sawyer, antics and mouth just shy of a badly trained monkey. Whitley's reeling off an agenda that makes my head spin, and I'm not even really listening; can't imagine how painful it is for those who are. Laney's all kinds of worked up inside, body language stiff and obviously on-edge, which I know is because she's worried about me. And Bennett.

Speaking of Bennett. On her return from the restroom, the man she's currently dancing with had inserted himself directly in her path.

And there's nothing wrong with that.

Of course Bennett's moved on, as she should. It's been years since my brother died, but to me, it feels like yesterday. Yesterday, that an elderly man, leaving the dentist (obviously too soon), crossed the median and sent Tate's vehicle careening over the hill, where he met his death.

I didn't go after the old man, his guilt immeasurable punishment enough, nor the dentist's office… because neither one would bring Tate back, only adding a battle on top of the one I was already fighting to come to terms with the loss.

That fateful day, Tate had been on his way to look at a house. A house he was planning to buy for him and Bennett as a surprise with the newfound wealth the gym was bringing in. The next step in cementing their lives together.

Bennett now owns both the gym, and the house. Two things, I *could* control, and did.

"Hey you." Laney leans in, hand rubbing my leg. "I don't like it when you leave me." She uses my earlier words against me in a sweet whisper, filled with love, at my ear.

"I'm right here." I continue the reenactment.

"No, you're not." This is the part where she says *"but you will be"* and ravages me atop the dinner table. I wait for it. "But that's okay. I'll be right here when you get back."

Damn… she has a way; her version almost better than my own.

I shake my head to clear the cobwebs of memories, doing my best to engage in the conversation and camaraderie surrounding me, laying my hand over Laney's, that never left my leg.

"So in the morning, we have a meeting with Pablo, the on-site coordinator. Laney, I swear, I asked for *miniature coral* roses, but what he showed me yesterday? Huge orange monstrosities! Don't you worry though, I thoroughly explained the error to him and it should be fixed by tomorrow. We shall see." Whitley finally stops talking to take a breath, and a sip of water.

"Way to be on top of that, Whit." Laney actually winces from the effort it takes to hide her condescension and I myself strain to keep in my laughter. "The size thing I get, but I didn't realize there was a difference between coral and orange."

"Retweet Gidget!" Sawyer booms, flagging over a waiter.

"Honey, not sure you can retweet something spoken, or texted, or basically... anything *not tweeted*," Emmett explains sweetly, everyone at the table laughing at her umpteenth attempt to explain this theory to him.

"Sure you can, I just did." He shrugs. "Oh, hey." His attention is now on the waiter at his side. "We're gonna need a couple shots of Patron Silver for everyone, mucho pronto *por favor*. Two right there too." He points to Bennett's empty chair.

"Certainly, sir," the waiter responds in *English*, the language even I, lost in my own thoughts, know he's been speaking all evening.

"Why are we doing shots?" Evan asks, a leery side glance slung at his wife... who we all know talks *more* and even faster (I know, seems impossible) when inebriated.

"Not because your woman is making our brains bleed with her fascinating lecture on the differences in the color wheel, if that's what you're thinkin'." Sawyer laughs, blowing a playful kiss at Whitley. "We're on vacation, why not?"

"I'm down." Zach high-fives Sawyer. "Bennett!" He turns in his chair and yells at her, cutting into her dance from across the room. "Say goodnight and get over here woman! Shots with your family!"

No way she'd ignore that loaded directive. She's quick to whisper a goodbye to her dance partner, accept his parting kiss to her cheek and rush back to *her family*.

"Consider them as good as shot!" She giggles, doing some mini-shimmy thing with her upper body then dropping down into her seat.

Apparently, I fail to hide my shift in posture, because Laney's hand tightens on my thigh and she bends her head to place a soft kiss right below my ear. "I have no idea what's going on with you, but please knock it off. We're in paradise, with our best friends, for the wedding of the century if Whitley has anything to say about it. Whatever's bugging you, it can't possibly be bad enough to ruin all that, can it?"

That's the thing, I'm not exactly sure what's troubling me, or why. And as luck would have it, Laney's not the only one keen to my mood. Bennett, perceptive as ever, leans up to ask, "Everything okay, Dane?"

"Of course." I force a thin smile. "Why wouldn't it be?"

"I don't know." The beautiful redhead, green eyes searching mine for the truth I've yet to decipher myself and she knows I'm not giving, purses her lips. "I can't think of any reason. Not one that'd be logical, *or fair*, anyway."

There you have it; she's Laney's best friend for a reason. No dodging either of them when they smell trouble, hypocrisy, or just plain bullshit. Although, Bennett used to say things a little softer, the cynical edge to her new since... well, let's just say she changed with the changes.

Bennett senses my discontent, and she won't be letting me out of an explanation for long. She may let it go right now in the interest of our audience, but it'll resurface for discussion—when *she* deems fit. Not a second before, or after.

"Shots are here!" Sawyer whoops, shattering the tension at the table. As the waiter places two shots in front of each of us, Sawyer lifts one of his in the air. "Get 'em up kids, Big Daddy bout' to make a toast!"

Big Daddy?

Praise God that most of the other patrons have cleared out of the restaurant. Much like his filter, Sawyer's volume knob is also non-existent.

Laney elbows me, shooting me her unmistakable *I'm in charge on this one* death glare, and I begrudgingly raise up my shot.

"A toast," Sawyer begins, using his free hand to dig a piece of paper out of his pocket as he stands.

"Oh, Sawyer," Whitley interrupts with one finger held up daintily. "The written toasts are saved for—"

"Whit, you're as pretty as they come, woman, but there's only one beauty that gets to boss me. Right, Emmy?"

He's lying; Presley turns the man to putty too.

"It's not very long, just let him." Emmett uses a helpless smile to plead with Whitley.

I'd never admit it out loud, but I'm kinda curious as to what he's come up with myself.

"Fine," Whit huffs, lifting her glass with dramatic flair.

"Now then, as I was saying." Sawyer bugs his eyes out at Whitley, then turns to make direct eye contact with everyone else, one at a time. "To our Crew, the best fucking group of people a person could ever want to know, let alone have in their corner. No one or nothing breaks us. No one trespasses, especially lil' punks named *Ride Her*, who I'm happy as hell to see wasn't invited to dinner with us tonight. Anyway," he clears his throat, "as another pair of our own come together in marriage, our circle, bond, only gets stronger. And I vow," he waggles his eyebrows with a wolfish smile, "vow, see what I did there? To protect that circle and everyone in it with all I am. Cheers!"

As each of us finish laughing and shaking our heads, we join him in tossing back our shots.

"That was very nice, honey." Emmett rubs his arm as he sits back down. "I don't remember it going *exactly* like that when you practiced earlier, but you kept the ad-libs to a minimum, so all in all, it was lovely."

"Yeah, I changed unite to 'come together.' No need to get all fancy. And the vow thing, just hit me out of nowhere, while I was talking. BAM! Good, right?" He asks her.

"Yes," she bites back her snicker, unlike the rest of us.

"What's his deal with Ryder?" Laney asks me under her breath.

"No idea, but I'm sure we'll find out, way too soon enough."

I stopped "shooting" after the first two.

Then again, I've always harbored some loner tendencies when it comes to a Crew bender.

Which is why I'm the only sober one in our party, and by party, I don't mean *'how many in your party this evening, sir?'* as asked politely by a hostess. No, I mean, any crazier and it'd make a good pitch for "The Hangover 4."

Thankfully, a quick chat and "generous" handshake with the manager later, we have commandeered the service of two employees and private use of the patio, the moon and strung twinkle lights setting an ambience that has me wishing it was Laney and I alone here.

I'm slowly nursing my Scotch, a bit more relaxed now, as I watch the show. The Crew women, especially when drinking and given free rein to the outdoor sound system, are some type of tropical storm all their own.

And just like every storm is different, so are these drunk females. Kind of like… I chuckle to myself at the thought… those seven dwarfs my Disney girl adores. First, there's Whitley—Dopey Drunk. She tried to do a sexy dance, on the table; Evan caught her mid-air when she cha-cha slid right off the side. Now she's trying desperately to make Limbo happen, except no one will lay across two chairs for her… and she can't figure out how to levitate them in the air, then lower them little by little, if and when they do agree. So basically, she's just walking around in a half-backbend for no reason.

Next, we have Sleepy Drunk, a.k.a. Emmett. I've watched her eyes close at least twice, but she springs back to life when anyone calls her on it, smiling warmly as she watches Sawyer enjoy himself. He's offered to call it a night several times, but Em keeps insisting to stay. She really is amazing; for him, and in general.

Laney is Happy Drunk, which makes *me* happy. She's having a ball, dancing, laughing, meeting Sawyer jibe for jibe and dropping by my lap every few minutes to remind me how Horny Drunk is Happy's close relative. She starts squealing in a pitch I seldom, if ever, hear from her when the next song starts playing. "Oh, my God, Whitley, it's y'all's song!" She springs from my lap and runs to Whitley, wrapping an arm around her waist, and motioning Emmett and Bennett over to join them with the other hand. The four of them conjoin and start swaying together in a wobbly, uncoordinated line, belting out the words to what I recognize as Evan and Whitley's wedding song; "Cowboy Take Me Away."

They all collapse in a snickering heap when the song, and caterwauling, are over, cheeks flush and each a bit out of breath.

"You couldn't have picked a better song," Laney says in a breathless, dreamy voice. "Evan, your cowboy, taking you away to that gorgeous house in the country."

"Right? I love that house almost as much as him." Whitley blows Evan a kiss.

"I seem to remember days when you hated that house." Evan laughs.

"Never!" She jumps up and cocks a hip, hand propped there in indignation. "I just got a little, tiny bit flustered with all the work, and the heat. My God could it have been any hotter?"

"No!" We all bark at once. The whole crew had left blood, sweat and a few tears on the threshold of the Allen home, everyone chipping in to build their two-story house on the land given to Evan by his lifelong friend Parker Jones. I swear it was at least 100 degrees every single day until the house was done. No sporadic thunderstorms, or God forbid, days of overcast. Had to be some sort of record.

"It was well worth it. The perfect place for Evan, and you, Whit." Laney gives her a one-arm hug and rests their heads together. "Evan always loved that piece of land, and Dale would be thrilled that he ended up there. The slice of country heaven was made for you two, to start a family, and be happy forever."

"Enough! No sappy shit," Bennett snips, breaking up the moment and standing.

"Here, here." Zach lifts his beer in agreement.

And that brings us to the last one: Grumpy Drunk. Bennett's *never* been the grumpy one, but again, Bennett's changed. More so than all the rest of us combined. Bennett used to be the one who looked at what others thought ugly and pointed out all the beauty we were missing. The whimsical girl who made optimism a habit. Not anymore.

"DJ Laney, put on something fun to dance to or I'm out!" Bennett directs and Laney quickly complies. Drunk or not, Laney *never* passes up an opportunity to run the music. "Zach," Bennett holds out her hand. "Come dance with me."

Once Laney finds a song she likes, she's out there too, dancing right beside Zach and Bennett. And of course, Sawyer joins her just as Emmett drops in the chair beside me.

"What are we gonna do with them?" She asks through a tired laugh.

I turn my head and give her the same smile of understanding I've shared with her many times before, the two of us sitting back and watching the shenanigans of our counter-parts a familiar spot.

"Same as always, Em. We're gonna try to be the voices of reason first, and when that doesn't work, have bail money ready. But above all, we're just gonna love 'em."

"Sounds good. Sounds real good."

Chapter 6

Trouble Always Finds Me

-Laney-

She texted me three times; one hour, thirty, and finally fifteen, minutes ago. Then she had them ring our room, twice.

Now, I'm gonna take a wild guess, and say it's her pounding on the door. Yup, definitely her—the screeching, quickly nearing dog whistle decibel, which would be great if it did make it there... cause then I wouldn't hear it—the defining clue.

"Baby." Dane laughs. "I think Whitley might need you for something."

"Hmmph." I pout from under the pillow I'm smashing over my head. Obviously, I'm aware he's not in the bed, and I don't even have to look to know he's also already freshly showered, shaved, dressed in some sort of sex personified outfit and he's read the whole paper while he ate breakfast.

Why are we not sleeping in on mornings we actually can?

"Can you just answer the door and tell her I'm sick?" *Not a total lie, my head and stomach currently fighting over who hates me more for quenching my thirst last night.* "She drank a lot more than I did, how is she even up right now?" I groan.

"Laney, it's noon. And her alcohol intake wasn't coupled with an already dire aversion to mornings. I'm letting her in, brace yourself, Sunshine."

"Laney!" My head literally. Splits. Wide. Open with her greeting. I highly suspect she may actually have a bullhorn in her hand. And is standing over me, rather than in the living room. "We're gonna be late, get up! I should *not* be the only one worried about this wedding!"

"Orange is orange, Whit! And from what I hear, it's the new black too! The world's gone mad I tell ya!" I wince; quickly realizing that yelling back may not have been the best idea. "You go pick whatever color you want, I don't care, promise. Besides, I gotta check in with my parents before I do anything anyway. I'd only be holding you up with my challenged sense of style." I start to rouse, tossing aside the pillow and cracking my eyes open inch by excruciating inch.

"Your parents and I had breakfast together this morning and now they're off doing a boat excursion tour," Dane helpfully chimes in with that pompous ass undertone he thinks doesn't make me want to strangle him as he heads for the door.

"Where are you going?" I sit up and flinch, a stabbing jolt of pain searing through my temples.

"Anywhere but here." He pivots, coming back to lean over me, hands braced on the bed on either side of me, and gives me a chaste goodbye kiss. "I love you, and I can't wait for the wedding, but I don't need to be involved in every last detail. You know how much I enjoy a big, juicy steak?" I nod dumbly, still half asleep, my head feeling even fuzzier with this odd line of questioning. "Well, I don't need to watch them go to the auction, buy, load, then butcher the cow in order to do that."

"Neither do I," I hiss at him in gravely low irritation, hoping Whitley doesn't overhear, and that he takes pity and doesn't leave me stranded with Suzy WedsAlot.

This only manages to earn his hearty laugh and another condescending forehead kiss. "Play nice, she's worked hard on this wedding. *Saved* you a lot more pain than she's inflicted."

"Didn't we order the wedding package?"

"We did. I'll let you ask her about that. I don't know how it all works."

"*Apparently*, neither do I."

"So grumpy when you wake up." He laughs at me again and kisses my forehead. "I'll see ya later, baby."

"Good luck," I hear him mumble to Whit on his way out.

"Do I have time—"

"No," she cuts me off, marching into my room and over to the dresser, flinging open drawers and hurling clothes across the room at me.

"Well can I at least—"

"No, hurry up, we're already late. One of the first things Pablo told me was that he appreciates punctuality. You've ruined that!" A red flush blooms over her face as she stands with her arms crossed, foot tapping out the beat of a diva in distress. "It's fine, I'll come up with a believable explanation, and just pray he forgives us."

Oh, you have got to be kidding me! Are those *tears* welling up in her eyes? I roll mine clear to the back of my head as I hurry to change my clothes; as fast as my hung-over state will allow.

I mean, God forbid we keep precious Pablo waiting.

Not that *we're* the ones paying *him* or anything.

About two, if I had to guess, hours later, and I'm finally able to take a full, deep breath.

I don't know where anyone else is or what they may or may not have planned. No idea as to the whereabouts of my phone. Complete lack of concern what time it is or if a search party has or has not been launched in my behalf.

Heaven. Just me, my poolside lounge chair, book I've yet to open, and a fresh drink on the table beside me.

I'd managed to give Whitley "the slip" somewhere between ivory versus eggshell table linens and scurried like a wanted fugitive into hiding.

Changed into a bikini, big, floppy hat and sunglasses in record time, I grabbed my romance novel and discretely made my way to the pool.

And I've been right here ever since.

The fact no one's found me yet has to be some type of divine intervention; payback for the God only knows how many torturous questions I endured, with feigned interest and smile, from Whitley and Pablo. A dangerous duo.

My theory is, Whitley's using this wedding to unleash all the repressed energy she *didn't* use on her own. She and Evan were married in Parker's barn. Seriously, I have to contemplate between floating candles or gel votives longer than one debates whether or not to be an organ donor, but people *sat on hay* and strained to hear the Preacher over the horses whinnying at her wedding! It was beautiful though, and I thought it was perfect. But I now suspect it was more a sacrifice on Whitley's part because it's what she knew Evan wanted.

And now I feel guilty for not indulging her enthusiasm with a little more of my own.

And completely disappearing… that too. Very sorry.

But not enough to get my ass up outta this chair. Let's not get crazy or anything.

Just when I flip over to my back, Karma rolls over me in the form of a shadow.

Maybe if I lie very still, they won't see me and go away.

"You can save the sleeping act, it's just me." I let out a huge sigh of relief at the sound of Bennett's voice and lift my shades. She's standing over me, snickering to herself. "Are you hiding in general, or just from Whitley specifically?"

"Sshh." I frown, my expression as close to authentic chastisement as I can muster… since I'm a phony. "If you say it out loud, it *actually* makes me an ungrateful, shitty friend. So I'm just gonna pretend I didn't hear you ask." I close and re-open my eyes, shaking my head and squaring my shoulders, the official sign of a do-over. "Hey Bennett, how's your day? Wanna catch some rays with me?"

"Well," she drawls, taking the lounger next to mine, as far from lounging as one can get without having an actual metal rod up their ass. "I have a better idea." Ankles crossed, one foot flicking non-stop, she chews on the corner of her lip.

"I already know, whatever you're gonna say next, my answer should be an automatic, unequivocal, no."

"But you still wanna hear it, dontcha?" She waggles her eyebrows, she-devil personified.

I act put-out, throwing in a loud, despondent sigh (so when I have to claim to have really fought her off later, I don't feel so guilty). "I suppose, let's hear it."

She's nodding her head before she even starts speaking. "I say we get away from the resort, go exploring the town, do some shopping! A girl's day!"

"Uh huh, helluva plan, B. I'm sure Dane won't flip shit too hard at the thought of just the girls wandering around Jamaica alone."

"What if we promise to bring him back some pot? I hear it's not hard to come by around here."

"Yes, why didn't I think of that?" I snap sarcastically as I roll my eyes. "As long as we assure him we'll stop and fraternize with the local drug dealers, I'm sure that'll put his mind at ease. Work *with* me, Bennett, not against me."

Nothing short of catastrophic, she throws herself on her back in the lounger, arms flying up and out. "One afternoon! I think we can manage! Shocking, I know, but I do live every day of my life by my damn self, like a fully functioning adult!"

"Easy, Ben," I say friendlier than I feel. I'm certainly not looking to be insensitive to the differences in our lives, a significant other at my side who watches out for me, but I'm also not about to sit silent while that other gets dogged either.

"Maybe we could—"

"I got this," she interrupts me, firing away on her phone.

Chapter 7

Not a Fan of Field Trips

-Dane-

After a round of golf, all us guys grabbed a table at the bar to have a beer. Which turned into several beers. The head on mine hadn't even settled before Beckett's groaning out his alert.

"Oh, shit, incoming." I turn to follow Sawyer's gaze at what, or who, ever has caused his warning, even though I know it's not my woman approaching. I'm well aware where Laney is, and that she's fine, I'm sure feeling better than she has all day. Despite her attempt to hide from Whitley under a huge hat and sunglasses and blend in with the crowd at the pool... I found her. I always do.

Laney never "blends in," and it's all the sexier that she's oblivious to the fact.

Seems I spoke too soon. Our post-game hideaway is being infiltrated by the women, Laney included in the pack.

"What the hell women?" Sawyer, obviously not wanting to get laid anytime soon, asks them.

"*Simmer down*, Fagger Vance." Laney pops off effortlessly. I'm not the only one who dies laughing, Evan spraying the drink he'd just taken everywhere.

"Damn Laney, very nice!" Zach holds up his hand for her to high-five. "Wish like hell I would've thought of it first."

Sawyer looks around, confused. "I don't get it?"

"*Bagger* Vance, the movie about the golfer?" I explain.

"Oh, yeah! Shit, that *was* a good one, Gidge." Sawyer smiles at her, respect for a great jab evident in his eyes.

"Thank you." My girl curtsies, then maneuvers her way onto my lap. "Did you have fun?" She asks me.

"I did."

"Did you win?" I'm surprised that wasn't her first question.

"We did, Zach and I."

"Atta kid." She does nothing to hide the pride in her purr before planting a hard kiss on my mouth. Her competitive streak isn't limited to herself; she loves it when her man beats the others in the group. I'd worry it was borderline unhealthy... if her reaction wasn't so damn hot.

"Anyway," Bennett's voice booms, causing Laney to startle and jolt back from our kiss. "We've got to get going, daylight's burning. Ladies, Zach, you ready?"

"Ready!" Whitley's at her side in a flash, beaming. Followed by Emmett, giving Sawyer a small wave. And lastly, Zach kills his beer and stands.

All of them now looking to Laney expectantly.

I am the only person here who doesn't know what's going on. *That*, I know without question.

Laney's stone still in my lap, waiting for me to ask, and I'm waiting on her to tell me.

And Sawyer's grinning for ear to shit-eating ear, way too excited over the drama about to unfold to have a dick.

"Oh, no, please, allow me," Bennett huffs, rolling her eyes with a flare that gives Laney a run for her money on the technique. "Dane, we're gonna go sightsee, shop, all the girls. And before you wind up in your alpha, bossy, protective hysterics, *Zach*." She curls her hand around his arm and flashes a satisfied smile up at him, "agreed to come with. So we're safe."

Zach's going with them?

What happened to his whole "exotic girls in the pool" agenda? Dozens of half-naked, bronze-skinned women prancing around screaming of invitation and... he's offering to chaperone shopping expeditions with four women of whom he has not a chance at?

And where the hell was I in the developmental stages of this plan?

"Damage is done then." I grin, confident my upcoming point won't fail. "Already one man tagging along, what's one more? Come on, baby." I help Laney up and out of my lap so I can stand, and when I do, she's dragging me away from the group.

"Babe." She rests a hand on my chest and looks up at me with wide, pleading eyes. "Bennett kinda wants to do something with her girlfriends only. Well, and Zach, cause we knew we'd be safer taking a guy, but he's not part of a couple. It gets hard for her sometimes, all of us *together*, and she's, alone."

How am I supposed to argue with that?

"I'll be fine." She cups my cheek and snickers softly. "You worry too much."

"Just stay close to Zach, alright?"

"Promise."

With a sigh of defeat, I take her hand and lead us back to our friends, less than thrilled with this whole half-cocked idea. "Zach, there's four of them. You sure you got this?"

"You know better than to even ask me that. Now if you'll excuse me, I need to get my shopping on. Ladies?" Zach holds out an arm to usher them away. Laney barely stops to give me a quick kiss before falling into line.

Once they're out of view, I turn and ask Sawyer and Evan, drinking their beers like nothing, let alone our women meandering off in an unfamiliar city, just happened.

Sawyer opens his mouth to enlighten me but Evan stops him just shy of whatever brilliance he was about to spew. "Let me take this one. Dane, I hear ya, strange place, they might get lost or whatever, I get it. But Zach is more than capable of lookin' out for them, *and*, they're grown-ass women. Can't exactly forbid them. If we were in Kuwait, I'd agree with ya. But we're not. So try and relax. Sit down, I'll buy ya a beer."

Unable to resist, Sawyer has to have the last word. "Look on the bright side, Kendrick. Of the four women, yours definitely has the best odds in the street fight you're imagining. Hell, mine's only packin' a sweet smile and calm personality in her arsenal. And Evan's? She'll try to sing the bad guys to sleep."

"This is why I asked that you let me take this one," Evan grumbles and shakes his head. "You're about as helpful as tits on a boar."

Four hours later and they're still not back. Laney's phone is sitting on the nightstand by our bed, so I know why she's not answering my calls or texts. And I'm not sure if Bennett and Zach have their phones, but even if they do, I'm well aware they wouldn't answer to passive-aggressively remind me they think I'm too overprotective of Laney. Emmett and Whitley's radio silence? No idea.

But I'm done sitting here wondering while doing nothing to solve the problem.

Thankfully, four hours and no return calls or texts was enough to bring Sawyer and Evan around to my way of thinking too.

"Track the GPS on their phones," I tell them both as we load up in the cab. "Worth a try."

"What?" Evan laughs.

"What, what?" I look at him exactly how I mean to, like he's wasting time.

"Track. Whitley's. Phone." I only just stop short of including condescending hand gestures as I repeat myself.

"Gotta say, I never thought this would be a sentence I found myself having to ever say, but, I don't have a tracker on Whit's phone, man." He stares at me exactly how he means to, like he thinks I'm insane.

"Don't look at me, you crazy fucker. I don't even know Emmett's phone number. I just tap her name that she programmed in there," Sawyer adds. "Damn phone's like working a NASA program. You're lucky I know how to turn it on."

So *this* is our plan? Sit here in the back of the cab like the Three fucking Stooges, no idea where to tell the driver to go?

Yeah, can't think of any reason why it won't work.

Except for the fact that our women are missing, IN JAMAICA, suddenly no one knows how to work a god damn phone and there isn't even close to enough room in this backseat for all three of us.

Anybody ready to start doing things my way, *the first time?*

Call me overprotective.

Call me crazy.

But at least I answer when you call me!

An idea comes to me. Maybe...

"Did you pick up any other groups here today?" I lean forward and ask the driver.

"Yah." He nods, answering in a heavy accent.

"Was it four women, one with red hair, one brown and two blond? And a big blond guy?"

"Yah." He bobs his head again, then turns around with a big smile... and holds out a joint. I realize I probably look like I need to calm down, but...

"Did you offer *them* a joint?" I ask, just as Sawyer reaches out and snags it from his hand.

Again with the "yah." At this point, I'm not sure if he's baked out of his mind, actually answering me or simply repeating the only word he knows over and over.

"Did they take it?" Evan asks him.

"Yah."

Okay, now I actually hope it's the latter.

"Can you take us to where you took them?" I hold out an American hundred dollar bill, and he's flooring the gas as he grabs it.

One death-defying cab ride later and I breathe for what feels like the first time in ten minutes as my feet blessedly find the ground.

Takes less than a second to deduce that I breathed too soon. My hands clench in fists and my anger threatens to boil all the way over as I take in the scene around me. Evan either feels the same, or picks up on the dangerous vibes coming off me, because he's quick to push my shoulder. "Let's start down this way, not gonna find 'em just standing here. Sawyer, come on."

Well don't I feel stupid for being concerned? This area isn't sketchy at all. And so what if we've been offered weed half a dozen times and a trio blowjob for the price of one in the first twenty minutes of our search… seems totally legit, right?

"Lighten up, Kendrick. You're a businessman, you should appreciate that she was gonna give us a good deal." Sawyer attempts some very ill-timed sarcasm.

I'd ask if he was high, but I already know the answer. Yes, he'd stopped someone on the street to borrow a lighter to partake of the blunt he'd gotten from the cabbie. Well, *tried* to partake I should say. Two hits and he called mercy, tossing it down on the ground.

"Sawyer, enough," Evan grinds out for me. "Situation's serious now, even I'm getting worried, which means Dane's about five seconds from completely losing his shit. This isn't safe and we need to find the girls. So help, or shut the hell up."

"Damn." Sawyer scrubs his hand over his face. "You're right, sorry. Okay." He claps, trying to convince himself he's suddenly clear-headed. "Let's do this, what's the plan?"

"We keep walking. There's three of us, so we use that to our advantage and miss nothing. I'll check inside the places we go by. Evan, you watch the other side of the road and make sure they don't pass us coming back up. Smoky, you keep an eye on the cabs in case they pile in one. And everyone keep trying their phones." It's the best plan I've got, and even I know it's a shitty one.

I text the group again, so damn mad I can barely type.

Me: Swear to God, if any of you are seeing this and ignoring it. Where the fuck are you? The rest of you can do whatever you want, but tell me where Laney is right now.

Evan: Whitley too. Enough is enough.

I look over at Evan, somewhat shocked. It's not often you find us on the same side of a matter, but even more seldom he willingly jumps in a group text.

He must see the surprise on my face. "Got your back on this one. Some real bullshit they've pulled."

"Me too, Kendrick. I'm not sure what they lace their pot with here, but as soon as there's only one of you, I agree with him."

Fucking Beckett.

Chapter 8

Now Trouble Found Me......... Sweet!

-*Laney*-

As I sit in this bar, trying to ignore the building lump of dread in my stomach, my brain throws out a random memory.

Back in high school, Kaitlyn put me in a similar situation as tonight... and her plan didn't work either. We were sleeping at her house that night and her parents had told us to be home from Parker's bonfire by midnight.

We'd both gotten caught up in the music, our friends, and lost track of time. When I checked my phone and saw it was ten minutes to twelve, I panicked, grabbing Kaitlyn by the arm and scrambling for her car. And then she stopped, as if not a care in the world, and told me, "No way we'll make it home in time now. We're already late and in trouble, might as well stay and enjoy ourselves as long as we can. Make it worth it."

It was a dumb theory then, and an absolutely asinine one now.

Shopping and lunch was fun, we really did have a great afternoon taking in all the sights, sounds and carefree atmosphere Jamaica has to offer, but now... not so much. Clearly, Bennett had made some last minute changes to our plans and forgotten to jot down the memo for the rest of us. Because when we all agreed to stop and rest our feet over one drink, I missed the not so happy ending where me, Whit and Emmett said we'd camp out in the corner for damn near two hours while Bennett danced the night away.

This bar is sketchy at best and Bennett's no longer even spending time with us, but I'm desperately trying to cling to my last shred of patience and support my friend. I know she gets tired of constantly hanging out with all the couples, thus the reason I'm still even attempting a smile and my ass remains glued to my chair.

But I'm not a complete idiot.

"Whitley, can I see your phone?" I hold out my hand as I ask. I'd left mine back in my room, and as much as I'd rather be forced to listen to "Uptown Funk" on endless repeat than the lecture I'm *positive* Dane has prepared, I know it's past time to check in with him. If *I'm* feeling antsy, weary of how long we've been gone, there's no doubt Dane's about to crawl out of his own skin.

"It's dead." Whit frowns, her aggravation not quite matching my own... cause it never does, but I can tell she too has had all the fun she can possibly stand. "Let's just tell Zach we're ready to go."

Zach's been a champ today, all four of us always within his sights, carrying our bags, he'd even paid for lunch. Even now, he stands only a few feet away, keeping himself close to our table, but his gaze is focused, and I mean zeroed in to red-dot pinpoint, on Bennett, dancing with some guy who'd moved in on her just as finite the minute we entered the bar. And I haven't quite put my finger on it yet, but her dance partner looks familiar.

"Yeah, see if you can get him over here and tell him, but I still need to let Dane know we're okay," I agree with Whitley then turn to Emmett. "Em? Phone?"

And in classic Emmett form, she chews on the corner of her lip and hesitates, giving me a look riddled heavy with guilt. "Bennett asked us not to talk to the troops, remember? If we call them, her night's over and we broke a promise. Shouldn't we let her have fun a little longer?"

"Em, you're a good friend, but it's not fair to the guys to leave them worried this long either. I'm not saying Bennett has to leave, she can stay all night if she wants. I'm sure Zach will stay with her. But I'm tired, and honestly, I don't feel comfortable or safe anymore. I'm just gonna tell the guys we're okay, and if Bennett's not ready to go, then I'll have them come get us. We're just sitting here anyway, and I don't know about you, but I'm afraid to even rest my elbows on any surfaces. Now, hand me your phone, *please.*"

I only added the "please" for prosperity. I'm giving her five seconds to comply before I drag her over this table and rip it right off her *person.*

As neutral as they're trying to play it, I'm not fooled, Emmett and Whitley fail at hiding their relief. They know as well as I do that they've both been waiting impatiently for me to take the reins and give them an out. Well wish no more ladies, I'm willing to play the bad guy.

But Emmett wouldn't be able to sleep tonight if she didn't at least try to compromise one last time. "As long as we tell Zach we're ready first and see what he says; not really fair to get the guys mad at him, like he forced us to stay or ignored us, when we didn't say anything."

"Agreed." I nod. "Zach!" I yell, seeing as how Whitley's "loud" voice has yet to get his attention over the noise. He hasn't done a thing wrong, and I definitely don't want the other guys misplacing blame on him.

My big mouth is more than enough and he immediately turns toward us and hustles to our table, keeping one eye on Bennett the whole time. Which makes me feel better, marginally. He really is able to watch two places at once.

"You girls good?" He asks.

"Yes and no. I mean, we're breathing and all, not stowed in the bottom of a boat being sailed into sex slavery, so yes. But we're ready to go, so no. And I'm willing to bet Dane's hit his threshold on us being gone."

"Alright, you three stay put and I'll go tell Ben we're leaving. Why don't you shoot Dane a text? I, uh, seem to have lost my phone or I would've already." He pats down his pockets as he fumbles through his explanation.

He's lying. And the narrow margin of comfort I was grasping onto tightly for the sake of sanity vanishes... somebody stole his damn phone! I narrow my eyes at him, silently calling him on his bullshit, and he averts his own immediately.

Uh huh. Definitely stolen.

"Great idea." I smile as though it was actually his. "You get Ben, I'll text Dane." I wait until he walks away, then look to the girls. "Okay, even Zach said I should text them. Everybody feel good about that plan now?" I hold out my hand to Emmett.

And while Whitley says yes, Emmett agrees by placing her phone in my palm, *finally*.

Emmett: Hey, it's Laney. I left my phone at the resort and knew you'd be blowing a gasket soon. We're fine, on our way back.

I should've just sent a row of lil' white flags. Is there an emoji for that? Cause I *know*, even if he's short of furious, he's *well* beyond slightly unhappy. Not that I can blame him. Jamaica's beautiful and the people couldn't be friendlier-*truly*, the accommodations offered, right on the sidewalk, range the gamut... but being out here at night, unfamiliar with the area, does make me uneasy. So when he comes back with exactly that reasoning, I won't be able to even attempt my way through a valid argument.

Dane: Where are you, specifically?

"Uh, either of you know the name of this place? I ask them.

"*Why?*" Whitley's tone reinforces my own sudden suspicions.

"No reason, just, Dane was wondering."

Emmett: Not exactly sure, why?

Dane: Why? Why do you think?

Emmett: You don't have to come get us. We're headed back. We'll be there sooner than you could find us anyway.

Dane: Don't be so sure. Now where are you?

"Anything? Guys, what's the name?" My voice is shrill and I'm starting to sweat in secret places.

"It was named after a bird, wasn't it? Pelican? Flamingo?" Emmett sputters.

"Stork? Eagle?" *Okay, Whitley's just naming off random birds now. Not helpful.* "Want me to go out front and look at the sign?"

"No!" Em and I yell in unison.

Dane: Waiting

Oh, he's just gonna love this response.

Emmett: We think it's a bird name, maybe Flamingo? There's a little guy playing a steel drum on the sidewalk and t-shirts hanging from the awning thing.

Dane: Don't' fucking move.

Psshhh, like I was gonna.

"They're coming here, aren't they?" Whitley asks, just to offload some of her nerves, she already knows the answer.

"Yep." I pop, searching the dance floor. "Pretty sure they were already on their way. Should be barging through the door any minute now. So you see, ladies, bombs had already been detonated *before* the great text debate." Enough small talk, I need to flag down Zach and warn him ASAP. I stand on the bottom rung of my chair and wave my arms like a lunatic while screaming his name. Right before I throw my arm out of socket, he notices and speeds up his steps our way, *dragging* a scowling Bennett behind him.

"We're ready, let's go," he grunts over Bennett's harrumph.

"Too late." I shrug, looking anywhere but at him. I feel bad; if they were already looking for us, they're already pissed...

Zach doesn't deserve any of this. "Boys are on their way, want us to stay put."

"Awesome!" Bennett's frown is now a huge smile. "I'm gonna dance some more then." I don't get a chance to tell her how "awesome" it's not, or that maybe she should stick around to field some fury with the rest of us, before she's off, headed straight for the same very good-looking, tall guy she's been dancing with all night.

I'm trying really hard not to think her inconsiderate. She doesn't mean anything by it, Bennett would never intentionally treat any of her friends badly I remind myself. She's just been single so long, she's of that mindset, no other half's feelings or concerns to consider when she's finally lost in a good time.

"They mad?" Zach speaks to me, but watches Bennett... which I also have yet to put my finger directly on. Naturally, Zach and Ben always tend to gravitate toward one another, the two of our group not part of a couple, but there's something's different in the air around and between the two of them, has been since today's little adventure started.

"Laney?" He asks again, interrupting my curious, wandering thoughts.

"What? Oh, yeah, of course Dane—" I stop... and decide to let the thundercloud of a man who just stormed in the bar answer for himself.

Well this should be interesting.

But on a happier note, I see Sawyer noticed the t-shirts outside. Although, I'm not sure wearing the tie-dye garment around his head like a doo rag is his best look.

And Evan; I'm not sure if the worry painted across his face is about us being gone… or us being found.

"Hey." Zach turns to greet the three of them as I wiggle in my seat, Dane's livid stare boring into me. "We were just about to head back. How'd you get here so fast?"

"Your phone broken?" Dane seethes at him, taking a step into Zach's space, and ignoring his question.

"Babe." I jump up and hurry around the table, inserting myself between the two of them. "Don't be mad at Zach. We didn't ask him to leave until just before I texted you, which he suggested too. His phone, um, disappeared, and you know I don't have mine with me."

Dane's heart is banging against my hand on his chest. He looks down at me, his eyes silently telling me that no amount of rambling excuses are going to calm him right now, then back at Zach. "*Somebody stole your phone right off you?*" He asks Zach with an underlying sarcasm.

See, I shouldn't have made eye contact with him, even though his were narrowed suspiciously and mine were flittering as much as possible, without being too obvious, in an attempt to distract him. No matter what, he can read mine like an open book.

It's a weird transfer thing, not so much phenomenal as inconvenient in our current situation. I pick up on what Zach's not saying, then one look, and I've told Dane too.

"You get *robbed*, and that doesn't say to you, 'maybe I should get the women out of here? Cause, I don't know, they could get robbed too! Or, somebody could steal *them*?'"

Mayday. Going from bad to worse at warp speed.

I start to interject again, but Zach's not having it, growling right back at Dane over my head. "I didn't say it was stolen, I could've set it down somewhere. And as you can see, everybody's here, *no one got stolen.*" That last part he says in a mocking sneer, obviously thinking Dane is being over the top ridiculous now. "You need to chill the fuck out, man."

"Five fucking people and not one of you has a functioning phone, *still in your possession?*" Dane's voice vibrates with its intensity and both his hands are now shoved back through his hair. I wrap both arms around his waist, desperate to calm him down, when Evan has the good sense to redirect the conversation.

"Whit, why didn't you call?" Evan asks her, *nicely*, arm thrown around her shoulder, apparently not as concerned with the world ending as *some people*.

I flick my gaze over to Sawyer real quick, wondering about his reaction to all this… and wish I hadn't.

Sawyer's not mad.

And Emmett might actually get pregnant from their reunion.

Zach answers Evan, but the anger contained therein is meant solely for Dane. "Cause she was out with her friends, having a good time, and knew she was safe with me! I get that one of us should've called, but get the fuck over it. The next one of you who *even insinuates* that I wouldn't take care of these girls with my life is going the fuck down. They're not helpless, or three years old, and you're starting to piss me the hell off."

Evan is keen to who Zach's actually talking to as well, over-smiling and keeping his response upbeat. "You're absolutely right man. Everything's fine now, thanks for looking out for 'em. So, we ready to go then? Where's Bennett?"

"Dancing," Zach grumbles, nudging his head in the direction of her approximate location, sounding more pissed about that than he is at Dane.

"Damn!" All heads whip to Evan at his excited outburst. "You know who that is she's dancing with?" He asks everyone, but lifts a brow at me in question and it kills me I can't fire off the answer to douse that smug taunt in his eyes. "Shane Holloway, third baseman for the Pharaohs."

I *knew* he looked familiar! Dammit, I so had that!

"No shit?" Sawyer decides to come up for air, or maybe let Emmett have some rather, joining the conversation. "Leave it to me people, I'll go round up Bennett." He puffs out his chest and throws back his shoulders, weaving through the dancing bodies.

Like Sawyer's ever sat still through a whole baseball game in his life! *What a glory whore.*

Evan groans and rubs a hand over his jaw. "Everyone's aware he's going to embarrass us, right?"

"Surely not," Dane scoffs. "The only real question is whether it will take more or *less* time than usual for his stoned ass to cause a scene."

Emmett lets out a gasp. "His *what* ass?"

"Oh, yeah, high as a kite," Evan confirms with a chuckle.

Well of course Sawyer's stoned. Was there ever any doubt that Sawyer would live by the infamous *When in Rome* motto?

"Are *you* high?" I look up at Dane, searching his eyes for any tell-tale signs.

"Oh, baby," he snarls as he stares down at me and winks. "Don't you wish. No, Laney, I am perfectly sober, and still mad as hell."

I know I shouldn't shiver, and my toes shouldn't curl at his feral warning. I'm also probably supposed to remind him that I'm a grown woman, who can do as she pleases and doesn't take kindly to threats.

But damn if I don't forget, suddenly more ready than ever to get back to the resort, and our bed... with my pissed off Caveman.

"Understandable." I gulp, stepping in to connect every inch of my front flush to his. "After all, I've been a very bad girl."

Chapter 9

Deep Sea Diversion

-Dane-

Laney's parents had somehow managed to remain pretty scarce, entertaining themselves, on the trip thus far. And not that I mind their company whatsoever, but the *one day* in as long as I can remember that I've slept in, and they're at my door at 8 a.m. Loudly arguing with each other in the breezeway over whether or not it's too early to wake us. Debate settled. Not only did they indeed wake us up, but if Laney, the textbook example of *not* a morning person, is jumping up at the volume of their voices, everyone in Jamaica must now be awake too.

Needless to say, Laney and I had a late night. If I'm tired, she's got to be exhausted, and perhaps a little sore in all the right places. And not by the same unsafe extremes, but I'm kinda hoping she tests my limits again... soon.

I can hear Laney doing about as good of a job as her parents at whispering to them at the door, and I really wouldn't mind another hour or so to recuperate myself, but I'll be damned if I ever let Jeff Walker see me slacking. So I get out of bed, throw on a shirt and some gym shorts and go greet them.

"Morning, you guys come on in."

"Babe." Laney tosses me a glance over her shoulder. "Are you sure?" *She wants another hour to recover too.*

"Of course, let your parents in. Just give me a few to get showered and dressed and we'll all grab breakfast together."

"Okay." I muffle a laugh at the tinge of disappointment only I detect in her reply.

After a too-short shower, unaccompanied by Laney due to our surprise guests, I'm dressed and walk out to the living room. "Are we ready?" I ask.

Laney smiles at me, ushering her folks toward the door that I shut then follow a step behind, listening as my girl catches up with them on what they've been doing.

"Don't worry Dane." Mr. Walker turns his head to give me *that look of his.* "I've got plenty of Florin to pay for the meal this morning. Did you know that's the common currency here?"

I refrain from pointing out that American Express Black is taken *everywhere*, simply nodding. "I was aware, but good thinking, sir. Thank you."

"Well, somebody's got to make sure we eat." He laughs, looking proudly at the two women.

Yes, because Laney and I have been scavenging the island for nuts and berries in order to survive up to this point

He's a prideful man, who raised a prideful daughter whom I wouldn't change a thing about, so I shrug it off. Set in his ways is all. Deep down, he knows he never has to worry about Laney being taken care of. And deep down, I know he's never gonna stop *reminding* me he expects no less.

We spend the morning and early afternoon with Jeff and Trish, but after a big breakfast and then hitting at least twenty gift shops, *in an entirely different section of town then last night*, Trish is looking worn and Jeff is quick to excuse them for a nap.

I'm thinking a nap sounds pretty damn good myself, but one step back inside the resort lobby and Laney and I are bombarded. Sawyer at the helm. God help us.

"There ya'll are! Go get your suits on, we'll wait. I booked us all a snorkeling lesson." I steal a glimpse at Laney, hoping her face says *I'd rather have a naked nap, save us,* but it doesn't. Rather, her eyes are ablaze with the excitement of adventure, which she never turns down. And they're all standing there waiting expectantly for us to join them, towels and beach bags in hand.

"Come on." Whitley steps forward, doing that half-whine, guilt you into it thing she does so well. "This is our last day of fun before we have to really grill down and get serious about the wedding stuff."

"We weren't already doing that?" I laugh at the way Laney's brown eyes double in size and her beautiful skin pales as she asks. "There's *more?*"

"Oh, stop." Whitley swats her on the arm and giggles. "You're so dramatic. You know we've barely scratched the surface. But you secretly enjoy every minute of it. It's okay to admit it."

Emmett and Bennett spring to Laney's rescue, flanking her on both sides. "Just go get changed and we'll worry about tomorrow, tomorrow," Bennett reassures her and Emmett nods along.

"I just—why does one buy an inclusive *package*, if *you* still have to do all *the packaging*," Laney mumbles, shuffling her feet toward our room in a daze. "What exactly are we paying Pablo for again? Assisted suicide? *Mine*? I'm making a valid point, right?" She asks no one in particular.

"Quite the crowd," Laney mutters as we approach the boat. "Is that Shane?"

Sure enough, I look to see Bennett and the ball player standing on the deck waiting for everyone else.

"Yeah, I invited him last night," Sawyer tells us. "Seems like a cool enough guy."

"Just because he's famous. *And you were stoned*." She mumbles the last part too low for anyone other than me to actually hear as she hands me her bag and climbs aboard.

Not sure what her grumping is about, but I don't have a chance to ask as Bennett launches right in to introductions.

By the time we're all on a first name basis with new guy, the diving instructor is ready to start explaining procedures.

The captain announces we'll be departing soon and Laney whips her head back toward the dock. "Wait, where's Zach?"

"Hold up!" Evan shouts, standing and pointing at the couple running down the shore.

Yes, couple. Zach isn't alone, his hand holding that of a very silicone-enhanced local woman. Not just *any* woman either, which is how I know she's local, and could've told you she's every bit a DD even with her still some distance away. I'm not the only one who picked up on her familiarity either; Laney leaning forward and sliding her sunglasses down her nose a bit, gasping at the confirmation of who we're watching approach... in a bikini instead of a uniform.

"What the—?" She asks the air.

"So I'm right, that really is—" Laney jabs a killer elbow in my side to cut me off, and maybe crack a rib.

"Yes, that's one of the housekeepers." She hisses low.

My scoff grabs Whitley's attention, but I play it off since Laney obviously wants this kept on the DL, snaring my girl's chin and kissing her hard and deep. But the commotion of Zach and date climbing aboard causes her to pull back, her eyes narrowed in on mine. "Don't say a word, you'll embarrass her *and* Zach."

I agree with a wink as she climbs off my lap and takes her own seat, the cockblocking boat captain making a comment about safety as he walks by... which I have to admit, I agree with him on.

So Zach's rolling around in bed with the maid before she makes it. Why's Laney so paranoid that anyone would have a problem with that? Not enough sleep, gotta be why she's on edge.

Small sacrifice to pay for nights like we just had though.

Zach introduces us all to Tia, the impatient instructor tapping his foot while we take our time greeting her, and once they too take their seats, we're off.

After we've had an overabundance of safety information—cause really, it's snorkeling, not shark feeding—and some time to talk as a group, I'm positive there's something more than sleep deprivation going on with Laney. And she's not the only one acting strange. Bennett's sitting with Shane, but her attention, like Laney's, is glued on the show, just a couple moves or digit slips away from a NC 17 rating, Zach is putting on. One of his hands is hidden behind Tia's back, the other between her thighs, and his face is buried in her neck. Not that I care... and Lord knows I'm trying not to look lest I be accused of staring at Tia's huge rack. Even though Laney should know better, I'm a proud card-carrying member of the Ass Man Society. No sense in taking any chances though.

What's starting to piss me off is that Laney can't pull her annoyed expression or focus away from them, and audition for a role of her own, with me. I've never gotten any play on a rickety excuse for a boat, bound for Jamaican snorkeling, and feel sure I'm being deprived of the full experience.

Luckily, Sawyer either catches on to the girls' fascination or my frustration, and slings out a line.

"You searching for something in there, Zachary?" He rips on him. "Cause I'm pretty sure if that's where she put it, you would've found it by now."

"So Tia." Bennett seizes on the interruption, her smile an ambush and one I know to avoid, pure ice behind the facade. "You live around here?" The poor, unknowing woman nods with a friendly, sincere smile that does nothing to deter Bennett. "Yeah, thought I'd seen you around. Housekeeping, right?"

And there it is... the bagged cat has escaped, joined by the flash of annoyance in Zach's eyes.

Tia's cheeks flush with the signature red shade of embarrassment and she clears her throat before responding, "Just part time while I save up to move."

"Why would you ever want to leave this place?" Whitley joins in then. "It's so beautiful here."

I pick up on the reassuring squeeze Zach gives Tia's knee, silently trying to tell her *just talk to the blond girl, she's safe.*

"I have family in the states. I'd like to be closer to them." She heard Zach's message, avoiding even peripheral eye contact with Bennett.

But... the redhead won't be dismissed so easily. "Really, where?" Bennett bites out.

What the hell is going on here? Laney's head is darting between the two like she's watching a very blood-thirsty ping pong match, hanging on every word. Shane sits silently, at Bennett's side but no parts of their bodies touch, staring off at the water, more than obviously uncomfortable.

Join the club new guy.

"Florida." Tia answers.

"Oh, that's not far from us," Whitley, as naïve as she is genuinely kind, makes the mistake of exclaiming. Both Bennett and Laney shoot her daggers.

Poor Whit. Even *Sawyer* has fallen silent at this point. If that doesn't say "shut the fuck up and be prepared to take cover," I don't know what does.

I squeeze Laney's hip and lean in to whisper, "Mind filling me in on exactly what the hell this is I'm watching?"

"So you and Zach might see each other again then, huh?" Bennett asks as Laney shushes me and nudges me away, much like she would a gnat buzzing around and breaking her concentration.

"Hopefully," Zach answers for Tia, pressing a kiss to her hand.

"Right." Bennett mumbles, eyes rolling to the heavens.

"I'm not far from you either," Shane says, pulling Bennett into his lap as the boat comes to a stop.

"Yeah, perfect." Is the reply she gives him, polite at best, and even that's a stretch.

Our gear's on and we're ready to actually do some snorkeling. No way I'm the only one relieved to escape the awkward tension on the boat.

Especially Tia. Girl might drown herself at sea just to avoid having to endure another ride back with this crowd.

I pretend not to notice Laney snagging Bennett's arm and whispering something to her. And when Bennett laughs and dismisses whatever it is with a wave of her hand, I'm hopeful that means my afternoon, with Laney, may be salvageable.

But no. My girl's still frumpy when she dives in and joins me.

"Alright." I wrap my hands around Laney's waist and pull her through the water, out of earshot from the others. "Tell me what's going on."

"Nothing. I just, thought it'd only be *our group*, ya know?"

No, I don't know.

Zach's brought plenty of dates around over the years and I can't recall any of them ever receiving the icy reception Tia did today.

"Are ya'll jealous of her tits? Cause baby, yours are so much better." I dip my face in between them to show her how much I really mean it.

"You did not just say that!" She shoves my head back.

"Not the first part, nope, you were hearing things. But the second part, absolutely, and absolutely true." I wink. "Okay, did Tia short sheet our beds and I missed it?" I grin, nuzzling into her damp neck this time.

"No." She giggles, squirming in my hold.

"Then why do you girls dislike her?"

She sighs, tilting her head to give me full access. "I don't *dislike* her, Ben doesn't really either. It's, well, it's a territorial girl thing you wouldn't understand."

I wouldn't understand territorialism? I invented that shit! I scoff, then nip my way up her neck to find her ear. "They're done ruining my day. Feel me?" I grunt, and push closer, so she can indeed *feel me.*

"Yeah." she surrenders in a heavy moan.

"That's my girl."

The water I'm treading for both of us as I hold her to me is crystal clear and the bright red scraps of fabric she's calling a bikini are taunting me. God damn but I could look at her forever. She's always been gorgeous, but now with a more womanly body, she's magnificent. Her breasts are larger, heavier, and her nipples are begging to poke free of their confines, the pebbled tips rubbing against my chest. Her curves are more pronounced, full and feminine, and her plump ass that I've always loved... even better. Wouldn't have thought it possible, until it happened right before my very pleased, eager eyes. I slide one hand down to grab more than a handful of that ass, watching as all but lust leaves her eyes.

"Babe, they can see us." She pretends to protest in a raspy moan.

"Hold onto me."

She curls her arms around my neck and her legs around my waist, perfect fit, and I swim us over to the more secluded spot I'd already been eyeing, dark and shaded by the veil of overhanging foliage.

"Can you see any of them?" I ask and she looks, then shakes her head. "Then they can't see us."

I find my footing on a rock ledge and make better use of my hands, lifting her just slightly out of the water by her hips. She knows exactly what I want, her chest already heaving as she arches it toward my face. But I tell her anyway, because *I know*, she loves hearing it, and when I get there, I'll find her all the wetter for it.

"Pull it down baby, both sides, now."

By the time I've sucked down her neck, she's got her tits out for me, pushed up and out by the material tucked underneath.

"Look at those." I groan, dipping my head for a taste. I tease her first, savoring the whimper that escapes her as I slowly trace a nipple with the tip of my tongue. "What's wrong, not enough?"

She's not the only one who likes hearing it. Through extensive training, of which I have enjoyed every second, Laney has developed quite the dirty mouth… and it's all mine.

She grabs the back of my head and shoves it harder against her right breast. "Suck it," she pants. "Hard." And I all too willingly comply, moaning my approval around her flesh.

And when I've succeeded in making her forget any petty, earlier concerns, and all her inhibitions, I slink my fingers in the side of her bikini bottoms and give her a lesson of my own: deep sea diversion.

Chapter 10

If It's Not One Thing, It's an Urchin

-Laney-

Despite the bumpy start, snorkeling turned out to be one of Sawyer's better plans, not that it had a lot of competition to crack the top of the list. Everyone seemed to forget the tense boat ride to get there and thoroughly enjoy the snorkeling lesson. Have to say, I really enjoyed my time in the water… and I saw some cool fish too.

In fact, we all had such a good time, that after the boat brought us back (still an awkward ride but less so than the first; I mean, we had nowhere to go but up) to the dock in front of the resort, the Crew opted to stay in the water. Lounging, horsing around fun, out of the heat. Oh, Shane and Tia stuck around too.

Of course that "fun" meant several rounds of "Chicken," because I just can't seem to ever spend time with my friends in water without challenging them. The men quit "trying" years ago,

nowadays just merely standing under us and serving as our base as us women go at it.

I still beat Whitley and Emmett every time with little to no effort, but Bennett's gotten better. Maybe it's her new, more aggressive side, or the fact that Zach's big ass makes an unshakeable foundation, but she puts up a fight… that I thrive on.

But Zach isn't her base today, Shane is, and that fact, coupled with *other* extenuating circumstances, has her *on one*. So she takes full advantage of the game as an outlet for her downright scary mood, and beats me twice. I finally call "mercy," which tastes like shit and shame coming out of my mouth, and things calm down, everyone doing their own thing.

Dane's happy with my forfeit, wasting no time pulling me flush against his gloriously wet body, rubbing on me in all the right places. He's looking around, no doubt to find us another secluded spot for some privacy, when a blood-curdling scream pierces the air.

Dane and I both jerk our heads toward the sound and find Bennett in obvious pain, crying and begging for help at the same time as she pushes people away, not wanting them to touch her.

"Bennett, what's wrong? What happened?" I'm somehow managing coherent questions despite my panic as I fly through the water to my friend's side.

"Something," grimace, "bit me," sob, "my foot. Hurts," Ben can barely manage to articulate. Her face is a pasty white, teeth grinding loudly and green eyes red with impossibly dilated pupils.

"Okay, I've got you," I assure her, bending over to pick her up.

"No, no, Superwoman. I'll get her," Dane says, but Shane, no Zach, make that… both, beat him to it.

"I'll carry her." Shane's adamant, but unknowingly mistaken, because by the time he turns his attention from Dane back to Bennett, Zach's got her cradled in his arms and is already halfway to the beach.

"Thanks, *bro*, but I've got her," Zach yells at him but doesn't look back, laying Bennett gently on the sand. "I've always got her."

I grin at that. Seems territorialism is a Crew epidemic.

"Left, my left, foot, oow," Bennett's wailing as we all circle around them, writhing in evident pain, Zach drops to his knees beside her.

"Breathe, babe. Try to stay calm for me, I'll fix it," Zach tells her in a voice I've never heard him use, the worry on his face in complete contrast to the velvety strength in his tone.

"Jesus Christ, Sawyer! *Why* is your dick out?" I screech louder than I mean to, but not a complete overreaction, seeing as how Sawyer's semi is out and looming over Bennett like a heat-seeking missile. You know, because we didn't already have enough going on.

"What the fuck?" Dane too asks him, head turned away from Sawyer's junk on display.

"Dude, you gotta pee on a jellyfish sting. Everybody just stand back, I got this. I piss excellence." Sawyer takes his chub in one hand, widens his stance and is all but urinating on Bennett when Evan has the good sense to step in.

"I'm sure you do, but put your cock away, Dr. Dumbass. It's not a jellyfish sting. See those little quills sticking out of her foot?" Evan points. "She stepped on a Sea Urchin. No amount of your excellent piss will help. But thanks for scaring off the crowd, gives us more room to work."

I honestly wonder sometimes what would become of our crazy conglomeration of misfits if it weren't for Evan.

"Oh, yeah, I read about this in the tourism guide." Emmett finds room for her sweet lil' voice in the chaos. "First, you have to pull the spines out, then soak her foot in hot water. We'll also need to get her something for pain and use ointment to guard against infection."

"See, Sawyer? Sound medical advice, with no private parts poppin' out," Whitley chirps in her *run along children and let the adults handle it* voice. "And thank you for getting, *things*, put away so quickly. Great job."

"What Emmett said, can we do all that *now*?" Bennett screams, her pain clearly increasing, and probably more than a little annoyed that Sawyer's impromptu peep show halted our progress of getting her out of agony.

"Yeah angel, we're on it. Just hang tough for me a little bit longer. Sawyer, go ask the resort for anything they have for pain and some ointment. Evan, get a hot bath ran for her in one of the rooms. Em." Zach tones down the harsh direction in his tone as he speaks to her. "Do I just pull them out with my fingers?"

"Yes." She kneels beside him, "the shallow ones for sure. The more of them you get out, the less venom's going in, which is what's causing her the most pain. But any deeply embedded ones, leave until we soak them loose in the hot water and we'll use tweezers."

Shane appears out of nowhere, kinda forgot he was still here to be honest, and squats down on the other side of Bennett. "Had this same thing happen to a buddy of mine when we were in Aruba. I'll take care of this, gorgeous. Let's get you up to my room, sound good?"

"Fuck no it doesn't sound good!" Zach speaks quickly before Bennett can, in nothing shy of pure venom. "Sounds like you didn't hear me the first time, when I told your ass, I've. Always. Got. Her. *Always* includes *now*."

"We gotta problem here?" Shane stands... about four inches short of what Zach will if he decides to, and bows out his chest.

"We sure as hell do. That *problem* is my girl laying here hurting while you waste everybody's time. As if I'd let you, a stranger, take her up to your room even when she's in the best of health." Zach actually cackles, a crazed warning in his eyes. "Shut the fuck up and stay outta my way or leave. You understand me this time?"

Shane laughs, you know the one, where a guy makes that *I'm gonna act like I don't have time for this shit and I hope you buy it* noise. "Tia." He looks at her, who I'd also forgotten was here (much like Zach obviously did as well) and holds out a hand to her. "Allow me to take you home, or wherever you wish to go, since your date's obviously not gonna do it."

Zach's face falls, telling me what I already knew. He feels bad. He's a wonderful man and would never treat a woman badly on purpose... but priorities prevail. "I'm sorry Tia," he tells her with sincerity. "I hope you understand."

"Completely. All of it." She grins. "It was nice to meet everyone. Feel better, Bennett."

Zach's attention is already back on Ben before Tia and Shane have even walked away.

"Sorry I ruined your date," Bennett grumbles.

Zach chuckles. "No you're not. Not any sorrier than I am that I almost beat your date's ass."

"Agreed. Now fix me!"

"Okay, I'm gonna start pulling 'em out. Dane, give her your hand to bear down on."

Emmett scoots out of the way and Dane takes a spot beside Bennett, grabbing one of her hands in his. "Do your worst," he teases her.

I count nine spines stuck in her foot, and six of them come out pretty easily. She puffs out a gush of relief with each one and I can see Zach start to calm down along with her each time, his hand getting steadier with every removal. He's working on number seven when Sawyer returns, handing Bennett two pills and a bottle of water, tilting her head up for her with a hand behind her neck so she can take a drink.

"What were those you gave her?" Zach barks at him, never taking his eyes off task.

"Fuck if I know dude, but a lady who spoke English said they'd work. Oh, shit, lookout." He jolts back, pulling Emmett with him, as Bennett turns her head to the side and starts violently shaking and dry-heaving. Thankfully, she doesn't actually throw up, keeping the painkillers in her system.

"Alright, you're alright." Zach soothes her, grabbing his shirt off the sand nearby and using some of the bottled water to wet it, wiping her cheeks and forehead to cool her down. "There's two spines left in there, but they look pretty deep and the skin around them is purple. Let's take you to the bath and soak those out. I know you're hurting, but the pills will kick in soon. You're doing great, precious."

She nods, but barely, pale and weak. He scoops her up in his arms, cradling her while being mindful of her foot, and rushes toward the resort.

I see Whitley meet them halfway there, on her way back out, I assume telling them which room is theirs where they ran the bath.

Zach's got it under control, like amazingly so. Maybe it was just the stress of the situation, sheer panic, or for the sake of comforting Bennett, but don't think I missed the several terms of endearment he used.

Or the way the muscles strung tight in his locked jaw ticked and the vein in his forehead throbbed when he used every ounce of restraint in his body to concentrate on Bennett instead of throttling Shane.

"Come on." I take Dane's hand. "Let's go gather up everybody's towels and stuff."

After a shower to wash off the salt and sand, which Dane actually did for me, all too gladly, we get dressed and go check on Bennett.

I feel bad knocking and making her get up on her injured foot to answer the door, but I needn't have worried, because it's Zach who opens it.

"Hey," he speaks softly, stepping back to let us in.

"How is she?" I ask, looking around and not seeing her.

Zach motions us back to the bedroom, where Bennett is sawing, no, make that super-turbo *chain* sawing, logs. "Oh, my God." I giggle, no longer concerned about *anything*, the apocalypse included, waking her up. "I was her roommate, and I assure you, that thing she's doing now, did not happen. When'd she become such a snorer?"

"Today." Zach sounds angry, but is gentle and concerned as he brushes the hair off Bennett's forehead. "Pretty sure those pills Sawyer gave her were actually horse tranquilizers. I've been laying here timing her pulse and listening to her breathing. Both seem fine, and she's definitely not feeling any pain. Fucking Beckett." He shakes his head.

Man, if we had a win for every time I've heard someone say "fucking Beckett," my softball team would be Conference Champs… every year.

"I can get one of the doctors on the island here," Dane says with absolute certainty; because he can. "Get her checked out, prescribed something recognized by the FDA."

"I think she'll be okay. And I'm not just real confident in what a local doc would give her either, if ya know what I mean."

Dane chuckles. "Yeah, I guess that's true. *Medicinal* marijuana probably covers anything from a hangnail to a detached limb here."

I clear my throat to end their little satire. "Now that we've got that settled, Zach, you can go. Get a shower, eat. I know you've got to be tired. I'll stay with her." I offer.

And I am *not* well received.

"Laney, you eaten?" I shake my head at Zach's question. "Exactly. You go eat, get some sleep and worry about the wedding. I ordered room service, and I'll eat it right here, same place I'll be sleeping."

"But—"

"But nothing. It wasn't a suggestion."

Dane growls low in his chest, which Zach hears and laughs at. "Save it, Kendrick. I've already taken lip from you once this trip, not happening again. Get your girl and go."

"You better tell me if anything changes, Zach. I mean it!" I point at him and boss.

He smirks at me and slants his head. "You act like this is the first time I've taken care of her. Pretty sure I got it."

The knock at the door gives him the perfect excuse to usher us toward it, *before* I can interrogate him on the other times he's taken care of Bennett. "That's my food. It's coming in, and ya'll are heading out."

"Come on, baby. You heard the man." Dane urges me out with a hand on my back and the hint of amusement in his voice.

Chapter 11

Three on Me

-Dane-

After an enjoyable morning of breakfast with everyone followed by some sightseeing with Sawyer and Emmett, there's only a few hours left before I can finally, truly start to brace for a sense of peace.

So when we return from our outing and walk into the resort lobby, I'm a bit anxious, but in an excited, ready to be able to relax kind of way.

That delusion sure was nice while it lasted.

Seeing Whitley at the front desk, in the midst of full-blown catastrophe, puts my hackles right back on rise, my build-up toward tranquility obliterated.

I know whatever I'm walking up on is definitely that of havoc based on several, undisputable indicators. One, Evan is standing slightly back from Whitley, head dropped and shaking slowly side to side in his universal sign for *God help me, but I'm just gonna let her go with it.* Secondly, Whitley's face is flushed a bright pink and the voice she's using to argue with the resort employee behind the check-in desk has taken on that helium-filled quality that only she can pull off without a balloon handy.

And last, but certainfuckingly, not least is the fact that Macie, one of the bridesmaids, is doing a piss-poor job of hiding out behind the miniscule stature of Whitley. *Yes, I see you.*

"What's going on?" I ask as I approach the scene. "Why's Macie here? Someone tell me something."

"Just a mix-up with her reservation, relax," Evan's quick to assure me.

"Oh, good, see babe, no biggie. Whitley can handle it." Laney talks fast through her huge, fake smile that's probably hurting her face, tugging on my arm to persuade me in the opposite direction.

Sawyer snorts out in disbelief for me, not buying the bullshit either. "Hey Daney, I get the feeling we're the only two assholes standing here that don't know something. Whadda' you think?"

And in another startling twist of events, I agree with Beckett. I look at Laney, shifting her weight from foot to foot, not meeting my eyes with her own, rather casting them at something fascinating just beyond my left shoulder.

"Macie, lovely to see you." I address the shrinking violet, forcing her to peek around Whitley and acknowledge my greeting with a shaky smile.

"Hi, Mr. Kendrick. Thank you, for, having me."

"You're welcome dear. But, I wasn't expecting you for several more hours. How are you here?"

"I, uh—"

I spare the poor girl and turn back to Laney. "Where. Are. Our. Children?" I ask with a subdued stoicism I far from feel.

"Not sure, around here somewhere." She shrugs a shoulder in nonchalance. "But I *do* know they're safe. *And adults.* So just calm yourself down right now."

"Wait, what?" Sawyer yells. "The kids are *here*? I thought they didn't land till later this afternoon?"

"You didn't tell them?" Whitley's eyes are bulged out as she asks Laney.

And now, my wife decides obstinacy is her best defense. "No. I didn't." She raises her chin defiantly and props both hands on her hips. "We trusted them to fly here, they flew here. So what if they landed a bit early? Not exactly newsworthy."

If she believed that, she would've been able to look at me as she said it. Which she didn't. "No big deal, huh? Then why not just mention it?" The restraint I'm still able to speak with amazes even me.

She arches her brows in condescension. "Do you think I missed you checking your watch every ten minutes? You know better, babe. No way was I letting you storm-troop the airport like an early flight was a matter of national security, *and* announce to our children that you don't actually think they're capable of flying by themselves."

"I—" Never mind, I close my mouth. No way is this bull-headed woman gonna draw me into an argument, which I would win, right now. Instead, I face Whitley. "Where. Are. My. Kids?"

"I hid 'em right where you could find 'em," Whit replies sporting a playful smirk, obviously proud of her smartass comeback. "Out by the pool."

How do these women possibly entertain themselves when not testing my sanity?

I make it to the pool in double-step, still not as fast as I'd like, and unfortunately, hear the parade following behind me. Whereas I like to sneak up on a scene, skirt along the edges—yes, spy—Sawyer prefers a *less subtle* approach.

"Step away from the baby girls in bikinis you horny lil' shits!" He screams, to… pretty much anyone currently inhabiting the entirety of Jamaica. "Presley Alexandra Beckett, what the fuck are you wearing? Get out of that pool and over here right now young lady! And *walk*, no running, or *bouncing*!"

And the kids are now amply aware we've joined them.

"Dad!" Presley jumps out of the pool, ignoring his specific instructions, and comes running over. Which yeah, I can see why he's having an issue with her "swimsuit"… and I am in complete agreement with him on the no running policy. Every man, *who's not in her family*, have their sleazy eyes locked on her. Sick bastards, she's a baby!

"Hi, Uncle Dane." She waves at me as Sawyer throws a towel over her. "Oh, hey, everyone." Her brows furrow, a confused look on her face as she greets the masses behind me… probably wondering why every adult she knows here had to bombard her all at once.

"P, not kidding about this." Sawyer points and motions up and down his daughter, "*swimsuit*. Gonna need you to wear something at least two steps above being buck-ass naked or I *will* kill every punk with a penis within a five-mile radius."

"Nanabug, you like my suit, right?" Presley gives Trish, laying close by on a chaise lounge, her best *puppy just seconds from being put down at the pound eyes,* begging for intervention.

Laney's parents, as well as Evan's, act as grandparents to all the Crew kids, except they call their group the "Squad," and protect each other just as their parents always have and will.

"You look beautiful sweetie, and certainly save anyone the trouble of using their imagination." Trish answers straight-faced, absolute honesty, with a bit of sarcastic humor to take the edge off—just like her daughter.

"Nana!" Presley's eyes well up with tears, and Emmett comes around the crowd to wrap an arm around her daughter's shoulders.

"Presley, sweetheart, it may be a *little* revealing. Especially when you knew your father would see it." Emmett talks kindly, a loving smile joined by imploring eyes, trying to soften the reality of her words.

And I'm out. Let them settle it. Not my kid, and I've yet to lay eyes on the ones that are.

Laney scurries to my side, wrapping a hand around my bicep where she embeds her nails in warning. "Don't you dare yell 'Three on Me.' I mean it!"

Shouldn't have reminded me of the brilliant tactic I've developed, and haven't had the chance to use in far too long.

Yes, when our kiddos were younger, trips to amusement parks, softball games, even school carnivals, became too much for me when there were three of them to keep track of in crowds, so

I came up with a plan. No matter where we were, rather than waste precious time searching the area, in which my blood pressure accelerated at alarming rates, or yelling out their names, which could belong to a number of other children, I'd scream... and I do mean scream... "Three on Me!" at the top of my lungs, unashamed, and my kids knew, they better find their way to my side immediately.

It became less embarrassing for them, and Laney, as the parents of, and the kids ours went to school or played ball with got used to it.

Yes, since the minute they were born, our babies have shared the same protectiveness to which Laney grew accustomed long ago.

And I make no apologies.

I scan the pool and deck area, searching through way too many bodies that all look the same, about to ready to scream the phrase they secretly love, when I spot one of them, my baby girl.

"Brynny!" I yell, waving an arm in the air. She hears me and turns, golden brown eyes like her Mama spotting me. *My angelic child climbs up the pool steps slowly, in a well-covering top and shorts suit, and walks, quickly, but a walk nevertheless, over to me.*

"Hey Daddy." Brynn goes up on her tiptoes, hands braced on my shoulders, to kiss my cheek. "What took ya so long?" She teases me. Okay, so I'm a tad overprotective of my children, I admit it. But if you had a stash of diamonds, you'd always keep them in the safest place possible, no doubt you would.

Well, my children are priceless.

"Hey, Mom." She hugs Laney.

And doing his job as per our agreement, the *only* way I'd been talked into allowing my 18 year old baby girl to fly to Jamaica with the rest of "The Squad," instead of right by my side, my son JT pulls up mere steps behind Brynn.

JT, Jefferson Tate, named after Laney's father and my brother, flew with The Squad and signed a legally binding document, (hell yes I made one), that if one hair on Brynny's head was harmed, I'd take his car and demote him at the family company… after his mother bailed me out of jail for beating his butt.

The Squad "just had" to make a stop in Miami to pick up Macie, the bridesmaid, who attends college there and couldn't possibly just fly over herself, a.k.a. the perfect excuse for a pre-parent hoorah. And Brynn really wanted to go.

Little girls—I'm a sucker. *What can I say.*

And she *is* eighteen; which I pick and choose when to acknowledge.

"Didn't know you were here," I growl, answering Brynn's earlier question. "*Your mother* didn't think that was pertinent information for me to know. *That's* what took me so long."

JT throws his head back and laughs. "Good lookin' out Mama." He winks at her, then quickly pulls that shit back in when I stick him in place with a few daggers. "I mean, sorry, sir. Should've texted you as well."

"Stop." Laney swats my arm. "Don't make them feel awkward, they did nothing wrong, and they know it'll hurt your feelings if they side with me, the one who's right, in front of you." She opens her arms for a hug from JT, which he doesn't hesitate to accept. "We're just glad you're here, safe." She kisses his dark head of hair, the same color as mine.

"We saw Nana, but where's Pops?" Brynn asks, glancing around.

Pops is what the kids call Jeff, and I know why Brynn's asking. The two of them are thick as thieves, because Brynn plays ball… for her Mom's team, and is currently praying her Pops didn't actually pack a mitt and ball for an impromptu pitching lesson while in Jamaica.

"He's around here somewhere. And yes, he mentioned it." I laugh and tap my precious tomboy's nose.

"I'm gonna 'plant and peel' that old fart one of these days!" She frumps, crossing her arms. "Stats don't lie, he looked at those lately? Huh?"

"As much as I love discussing softball, every second of every day, the parentals have arrived and I'm off duty. See ya," JT salutes the three of us and all but runs away, eyeing a few ladies laid back in lawn chairs as he does so. My son, just turned twenty, lacks nothing in confidence.

Two down, one to go.

"Where's your sister?" I finally ask Brynn.

"Right behind you." I hear the sweet giggle from behind me and spin, just as taken with her now as I am every time I look at her. Our oldest daughter, Skylar, or Sky as most call her, is the mirror-image of her mother, with the headstrong attitude to boot, and yet, so frilly, they couldn't be more different. "How you like Jamaica, Daddy?"

"Sweetheart." I take her in my arms and hold on for dear life, with the same amount of strength it always takes to accept how grown up she is now, twenty-two years old, mixed with the tender care with which I held her for the very first time. No need to rehash the mix-up on their arrival, I just enjoy holding her; I don't get to do it near often enough these days.

"My turn." Laney nudges me out of the way and wraps her arms around our oldest.

And that's all of them; Skylar, JT and Brynn, the best three things Laney Jo ever gave me, besides herself of course.

Funny how things work out. It took me the longest of all the Crew pairs to convince Laney to marry me. Yes, even Bennett and Tate had definite plans before we did. And while Laney never quite outgrew her "tomboy" ways and swore up and down she wasn't maternal and didn't want kids… she honored me with the three most glorious ones to have ever been born.

"I have a mud bath and mani/pedi in thirty-minutes, but then dinner, as a family?" Skylar asks, dragging me out of my musings and back to the present. "And yes, Brynn, I made you an appointment too. You're a girl, I promise. You're coming. Lord knows we'll have to triple-tip the poor sap who gets stuck working on your cleat feet." She shudders, but with a smile; she never misses one of her sister's home games. Never.

"Sounds wonderful, all five of us together for dinner." I try subtleness; which has *never* worked for me.

"Daddy!" Skylar glowers. "Make the reservations for everyone, because you're going to be nice Daddy. Right?"

"Of course he is, honey," Laney answers for me, digging those nails in my arm again.

"I'll take care of it." I sigh. "Just figured it was worth a shot." I shake my head, hug both my daughters and turn to go with my wife, but Brynny tags along with us.

"So." I start, as leisurely as our stroll. "Why didn't that Ryder kid come with the rest of the Squad?" I purposely didn't mention it around Skylar, the worrier.

"He couldn't afford the extra flights for the stop in Miami, or the food, hotel and stuff that went with it. Why?"

"Just curious, seemed odd is all. And he's walking with Presley down the aisle, correct?"

"You're a terrible fisherman, Daddy. I don't know all the twists and turns at play, but even if I did, not my stories to be tellin'." She watches my reaction from the corner of my eye, then takes my right hand, the left entwined with Laney's.

"Any clue why Sawyer'd have such a problem with the kid?"

"No, but if I had to guess, I'd say he's jumping to conclusions. Just because you walk down the aisle with a certain guy in the wedding party, doesn't mean anything's going on. I mean, I'm paired with *my brother!*"

Laney and I both laugh at that one, not only because Brynny visibly shuddered as she said it, but because she's right, and Beckett's torturing himself for no reason. The latter bringing me endless enjoyment.

And one last cast at information, I change baits. "And Skylar was alone just now because...?"

Laney rib-checks me just as Brynn laughs this time, *at* me I'm sure. "Because she brought about seven bags that weren't to be trusted to bellhops, *and* she wanted to know *exactly* where she'd be staying. Make up whatever reason you can handle in your head for that one, the real one would send you into orbit. But trust me, she was being taken care of. Your kids are all here, safe and well loved. *That*, I know for sure, and swear to you. Good enough?"

"Yeah." I smile, squeezing her hand in mine, banishing all thoughts that might send me on a killing spree, rather focusing on the fact that my baby girl's unashamed to hold her old man's hand in public.

Why would I waste worry on anything else when I have that?

Chapter 12

What's Bigger Than That?

-Laney-

Before dinner, Dane and I take a walk along the seashore. On one hand, I know he's wound a little less tight now that our kids are here with us, safe and sound, but it's also an in-his-face reminder of upcoming events that are closing in fast, too fast for Dane to possibly be coming to actual terms with them quickly enough to be ready for their arrival. Maybe on the outside he appears to be holding it together, but on the inside? There's a cyclone of worst-case scenarios the likes of which Kansas has never seen brewing. I know him too well to kid myself into foolishly believing otherwise.

It took a little searching, but we manage to find our very own cove, set off from the shore; no crowd or noise, just enough seclusion to sit and simply stare out at the pristine water, reflecting… neither of us urgent to speak, but both dealing with so much swirling inside, knowing that saying it aloud would give it escape, releasing the weight of carrying it solely.

"You feel better laying eyes on all your children, Caveman?" I ask to the water, keeping my back to him.

"I do." He finally joins me on the sand, sitting at my back, contouring his arms and legs around me with his face nuzzling into my neck. All these years, and he still makes me feel coveted, desired, with every single touch. It may sound cliché, but it's a risk I'll take, cause it thrills me to no end being certain that my husband craves me as much today as he ever did.

And now that I know he's good, well, better at least, and I too have gotten my breather, I welcome the zing that erupts through me whenever he's near.

"Quite the detour you took here, baby. Any particular reason for the needed privacy?"

"I didn't figure you'd mind." I turn my head to kiss the corner of his mouth and when he demands more and takes mine fully, no need to beg entrance, I respond in full submission and a heady whimper.

Our tongues tangle in synchrony, weaving together in the solace and security we both need to be reassured of.

When we're both sated and feeling reconnected, and with the taste of him still on my tongue, I look back out to the water and sigh. "Do you remember when we were their age? Our wedding?" I whisper; unsure myself if it's melancholy or nostalgia contained therein.

"Of course I do, every second, every detail." His confident words heated on my skin.

"Oh yeah? Wanna make a wager that I can stump you?"

"Try me, baby." He laughs. "What's the bet?"

S.E. Hall

Never let me loose in a casino, I have a problem with betting. The struggle is indeed real.

"If I win, you have to spend some one on one time with Judd while we're here. Just you and him; friendly round of golf, lunch, whatever."

"And if I win?" He hums, skimming the tip of his tongue along the crevice where my neck and shoulder join, slinking the thin strap of my dress down to lick behind its path.

"What do you want?" I purr, head back and eyes closed, unconcerned with whatever the answer.

He moves my hair aside now and devours his way down my neck, leaving a trail of moist warmth in his wake. "I want to fuck you in the sea tonight." He grunts as I feel him harden against my ass; our spark as hot and live as ever.

"Deal," I agree readily, winner either way. I ask a hard one right out the gate. "When did I finally agree to marry you?"

"The sixteenth time I proposed, on the pier in Emerald Isle. We'd just finished dinner, you had the sautéed bay scallops and were wearing the red dress I gave you that night. You said, 'I told you when I accomplished all the goals I had to do alone, I'd marry you. I've graduated and got the coaching job I wanted, so Caveman, tonight, my answer is yes!' Then I slid the ring on your trembling finger and carried you back to our condo. Your dress unzipped down the side, no bra, and I told you to leave the black garters on." He licks behind my ear as he groans out the story, pulling me tighter against him, rigid length taunting my ass ever more so. "I let your hair down, pulled those little black panties to the side and took you from behind, bent over the dresser. Sound about right?" He torments, tugging lightly on my earlobe with his teeth, digging his fingertips into my hips.

112

"Uh huh." I gulp, my focus divided between the building desire scorching through me and breathing. "Our wedding, what—" I begin, but he cuts in.

"Your something new were the earrings your parents bought you. Old, your "D" necklace. Borrowed, Whitley's diamond hair pin. And blue," he snarls, but a small laugh sneaks its way in, "was a picture Sawyer drew of his balls since Em was ovulating, putting him out of commission for a while. Under your dress." I feel his thin shiver, "was all white lace. And you took it off, slowly, by yourself so I wouldn't rip it. Which I would have. Then you undressed me, lay down on your back in the bed and held out your arms. You said, 'I want my husband to love me, soft and slow.' I've never seen you look more beautiful than in that moment. The anticipation in your eyes, the tiny quiver on your lips. Like you could already feel how different it would be, what it would mean."

He remembers *everything* about me and it's all I can do to keep my tears at bay, hearing how each detail I hold precious truly means as much to him. Thank God Whitley loves planning weddings, she'd made it the perfect day. But no time to reminisce and get all teary-eyed now, I *do* have a bet to win here, so let's see if he pays attention to anything else in the room. "Go down my maid of honor and bridesmaid line, in order." I challenge with a confident air.

"Bennett was your maid of honor, then Whitley, Emmett, Hayden and Samantha." My mouth agape in utter shock, he laughs, sliding his hands up to cup my breasts. "Baby, you're riding in those waves tonight. Give it up," he growls.

"One more." I grasp for victory, even though…. I no longer want to win. "Our honeymoon, when the alarm we didn't set went off, remember?" I snicker. Unable to remember ever being more pissed off, exhausted from the best day of my life and wanting nothing more than to bask in our entwined bodies, lying in bed as husband and wife for as long as possible, an alarm we didn't even set had startled us awake. "What song came blaring out?"

"I'd Rather Go Blind," he boasts.

"You know how many times that song's been remade? Please be more specific." I force my lips in a serious, straight line. Gotta make him work for the win.

"Sydney Youngblood version. I know, you're a Side B girl, baby. I've learned to pay close attention."

"Fine, you win." I pout and turn to straddle him, running my fingers through his dark hair, touching our noses together. "Think you can navigate your way around the important things in only the moonlight?"

"Sure of it, baby." He winks. "Think you can hold on tight and take all I give ya?"

I nod just before he's kissing me with all the heat and exploration of the first time.

When I pull back to catch my breath, he holds my gaze. Mirth shining at me from his chocolate brown eyes. "Let's get this dinner over with, then tonight, you're mine. We gotta christen the Caribbean Sea."

"And?"

"And maybe, if he doesn't piss me off, I'll invite Judd to some golf tomorrow."

My Dane... even when I lose, I win.

We really should've opened this meal with a prayer. And stopped every few minutes to say another one, just for good measure. Cause Lord knows—no pun intended—divine intervention is our only hope at this point.

Too many people at one table only increases the odds of at least one show-down, and now that Evan's parents and Blaze finally flew in and have joined us, our dinner party is in the double-digits. Bet on a showdown for sure.

"I can't decide where to look." I duck my head to Dane's ear and whisper.

"We're gonna have to split it up." He laughs hollowly, wired by the same palpable tension I feel simmering to a boil around us. "I'm thinking, you keep an eye on Sawyer, and I'll watch Ryder. Lil' too smiley at our Brynn, *fucker*."

"Sawyer? No, I always have to watch him! That's a full-time job, I won't have time to focus on Zach and Bennett."

This is the first appearance the two of them have made all day. TLC, my ass. Her foot isn't *that* hurt.

My poor husband, he just stares at me much like I'd guess it'd look if I were to announce I'm pregnant again, dumbfounded. He has no idea all the irons at play in tonight's fire.

"So, *Blaze*." Oh, shit, Sawyer's talking! I flip my head that direction, hoping I can stop the train before it wrecks. "What the hell kinda name is that anyway? Your parents actually chose that, or is it just some 'badass shit you go by?'" Sawyer sneers as he uses air quotes.

"Dad!"

"Sawyer!"

Presley and Emmett both chastise him as Bennett snickers.

But Blaze, apparently a friend of the kids', whom I've never met, which is odd if he's important enough to some or all of them to be a part of the wedding party, just leans back in his chair and chuckles in a deep, self-assured timbre. Sawyer zeroing in on him was inevitable; gotta be like looking in a mirror. The kid is huge, all muscle, covered in tattoos, dark hair close-cropped to his scalp and cocky ego emitting off him in an unavoidable cloud.

"What it says on my birth certificate," Blaze responds, left side of his mouth tipped in arrogance.

"Ah, so your parents must've borrowed the 'what *not* to name your kid' book from *Ride Her's* parents," Sawyer zings back.

Thank God the four grandparents are seated together at the end of the table, and I'm praying, can't hear the shit show unfolding.

"Ryder's a great name, and no one even thinks to pronounce it that way."

Brynn, yes, *Brynn Kendrick*, actually corrects her uncle, albeit in a quiet, hesitant voice and while staring down at the table, but still… completely out of character for her.

I glance at Dane, wide-eyed and as surprised as I at our baby's less than bursting outburst. And then I hear the growl, building in intensity and volume as it rises all the way from his toes to his chest and follow where his eyes have strayed.

To Ryder, smiling across the table at Brynn like she's the most precious thing he's ever seen.

Can't argue with him there.

"Fine, *Ryder*, you're off the hook. Can't piss off my Brynny." Sawyer grins at her lovingly, then flashes a smug version of the same at Dane. "So then Blaze, all you. Who the hell are you and why are you here? And late."

"I need more bread. Who has any left in their basket?" Bennett cuts in out of nowhere, madly searching every basket on the table.

"H-here." Emmett passes one to her, a smile of... gratitude, I think, on her face.

"Didn't work, ladies." Sawyer's sneer aimed at the kid now bares his teeth. "Asked you a question, Blaze."

I jam my knee into Dane's, the glass and silverware on the tabletop clattering. "Do. Something." I grunt out the side of my mouth.

He quickly stands, clinking his knife against his goblet. "I'd like to propose a toast."

Everyone falls silent, impending doom forgotten at least for now, and focus on Dane. I notice a little color returns to poor Emmett's face, while she rubs Presley's shoulder, and Whitley no longer appears seconds from tears. My son, however, looks disappointed, ready to watch more fireworks, for which I will ream him later.

Dane clears his throat and I peer back and up at him. So dapper in his black suit, commanding authority in the sexiest ways. My small sigh must find sound because he tips his head down to me and winks before continuing.

"I'd like to thank each of you for being here, to join us parents and grandparents, as we watch two wonderful young people we all love begin the blessed journey of loving each other for the rest of their lives. My beautiful Skylar, my first-born child, who I never imagined would ever be able to find a man worthy of her." He takes a deep breath, an almost indecipherable shake of his head, "has done just that. Truth be told, it happened a long time ago, it just took me longer than her to figure it out. There was this *one* little boy, who just wouldn't go away. Every time I turned around, there he was, right beside his 'Sky Sky.'"

We all laugh at the memory, that sweet little brown-haired angel, in his cowboy boots and hat, always right behind her, calling her "my Sky Sky."

"I think I knew I'd lost the battle the day my frilly princess, decked out all in pink and plastic high-heels, begged me to take her to buy a fishing pole and worms. I held out hope it'd only be the one trip, she'd have a miserable time, run home and crawl on my lap and stay there forever. But that didn't happen. And then, a day I'll never forget did. That one afternoon a beat-up pickup truck stopped in my driveway, and a young man all too familiar walked up to my door. Only this time, he didn't call me 'Uncle Dane,' nor did he ask me if JT was home. No, this time he shook my hand and called me 'Mr. Kendrick, sir.' And he asked if he could date my daughter."

I dab under my eyes with my napkin, and catch every other woman at the table doing the same. Except Skylar. Skylar's smiling from ear to ear, leaning against him, one arm up for her hand to curl back and cup his cheek.

"Well." Dane chuckles, "since Skylar had already heard him and came flying through the door squealing, I had to say yes. But," he makes direct eye contact with the young man, "I would've said yes anyway."

"Oh, Daddy." Skylar now sniffles, her words a mere wisp, as her fiancé draws her closer against his side.

"Judd Allen," Dane states, and somehow, conveys his veiled directive since Judd lays a soft kiss on Skylar's head and stands as though asked to. "I love you son. Loved you since the day you were born, to two of the finest people I know, who love my daughter just as Laney and I do you. I've watched you adore my princess since the day you could both walk and talk, effectively communicate and all."

Another wave of hushed laughter from all.

"I couldn't be more pleased that it's you, the only one who can put my favorite of her smiles on her face. But just remember boy." He lifts one brow, "I loved her first. Fiercely, unconditionally, and without end. At any cost. I expect nothing less from the man who will love her last."

That's it, I lose it, blubbering into an even bigger mess than Whitley.

Dane's eyes glisten a bit and his final words come out choked as he raises his glass. "To Judd and Skylar."

"To Judd and Skylar," we all mimic and toast.

My daughter is marrying Evan's son.

That's... what's even bigger than full-circle?

Chapter 13

More Than Words

-Dane-

After we'd finished dinner, Evan and both grandfathers also rising to give a toast of their own, and too many hugs goodnight to count, I'd made sure that all my children had plans of their own. That *didn't* include a late night swim at sea. Or being anywhere near the water for that matter. Once I had that confirmed, I proceeded to drag my wife in that exact direction.

"Dane, don't we need our suits?" Laney giggles, trying to navigate the walk in the dark, taking way too long in doing so for my liking.

"Nope." I stop and turn, hooking her behind the knees and throwing her over my shoulder. I've been thinking about cashing in on our bet all evening, my dick in a perpetual state of painful hardness under the table the entire meal.

"Oh, my God, you're making a scene. We're gonna get caught and arrested. Won't that make a lovely wedding memory for the kids." She tries to sound appalled, but the laughter dancing behind her words betrays her. Supposedly, you're expected to start acting "older" at some point in life, but Laney refuses, and this is one thing I happily follow her lead on.

I will never grow tired of Laney's youthful spirit, the fact that she jams her music louder than our kids and actually thinks she raps better than… whoever the hell she listens to. And I will *never* stop fucking her, each and every chance I get it, any and everywhere, like a randy teenager.

"Bet's a bet, baby." I set her on her feet when we reach the water, purposely choosing a secluded spot behind a large boulder, to shelter us from view. "You lost, now strip for me."

"D-Dane." She looks around, checking for any possible spectators.

As if I'd ever let anyone see my wife naked.

"Naked, now." I wink. "Gimme a show, sexy."

Too obstinate to break eye contact, she boldly holds my blue, desirous pair captive with her own honey brown set as she opens her shirt, one button at a time. My tongue glides across my bottom lip, impatient for a taste of the sweet flesh she's revealing. And finally, there it is, my North Star, the single freckle in the middle of her chest that I've loved since the first time I saw it. If I can see it, I always know I'm in the right place, or at least headed that direction.

She shrugs her shirt off her shoulders and stands waiting, yearning for my next explicit instruction, the fire in her eyes unmistakable.

"Now the bra." I toe off my shoes and socks blindly, not daring to interrupt my view.

She reaches around her back and undoes the clasp then holds the loose fabric in place with both hands, just begging me to seize control. Which I'm inclined to do more often than not, but tonight, tonight I want to be provoked and *lured* into taking her.

I slant my head and give her a suggestive grin, letting her know the next move will be hers, and I will wait for it.

Biting the corner of her lip, she lets the silk fall, arms then dropping to her sides. I harden even more from the sight, high firm globes topped with pebbled pink tips, bouncing for me with her labored breaths. My mouth literally waters to suck one in and play with it, but still, I pace myself.

"Love your tits, gorgeous girl." I reach down and flick open the button on my pants then unzip them, giving my rock hardness some breathing room. "Love that ass of yours more though, so show me. Keep going."

She slowly starts to work on her own pants as I do the same with my shirt, my chest bared by the time that she stands before me in only a meager piece of blue lace. Down to just my boxer briefs, I pull myself out, tugging up and down my cock with a tight grasp.

"Come here." I groan. Watching my hand in fascination, she walks toward me. "You do it for me. Stroke it, baby."

When her tiny but firm grip wraps around me and squeezes before starting to glide along my steel length, I grab both sides of her flimsy panties, where the lace sits on her curvy hips, and with one twist then yank, have them ripped off her body. Without having to be told, she releases me and drops to her knees, pushing my boxer briefs all the way down my legs where I step out of them.

My dick bobs toward her mouth, right there and begging to be filled. "Take me in your mouth. Suck me, Laney." She bends her head forward and wraps her lips around the head, running her tongue under the ridge there. "Fuck." I groan. "Good girl, just like that."

My woman can suck a mean cock. I taught her that. But she's too good, and I have bigger plans, so I stop her, pulling gently on her hair.

I'm done with the thrill of foreplay, ready to fill more than her mouth. I reach one hand down for her to take, helping her to her feet and leading us to the water.

It's nice and warm, complete darkness but for the moonlight. I grab under her ass and seamlessly, my woman curls her arms and legs around me.

I swim us over to the long pier that stretches out into the water and place a hand on her head, careful with her as I guide us underneath it. I push her back against one of the wide, wooden base poles and warn her. "Hold on," I hiss with fading control, needing to be buried in her more than I need to breathe.

"Mmm," she purrs as she curls her arms tighter around my neck, muscular legs ringing around my waist, squeezing her thighs tight into my sides. "Love me, babe."

"I do love you. But right now, I'm going to fuck you. Hard." That's the only notice I give her before I slam my dick home through those warm, wet walls of hers, made just for me. My head falls back and a sound I don't recognize resonates from deep within me from the sensation. She always feels so damn good, *mine*, an ideal fit. That tight pussy, I never stop wanting, constricting around my cock from the second I get it in her.

S.E. Hall

I know men operate under some myth that sex isn't all that great in water, the conduciveness of water not as fluid as you'd like, but when the pussy you're in is dripping and ready for you, everything slides just as smoothly as it should. And Laney's cunt sucks me in greedily, flawlessly, the natural lubrication of her want for me silky perfection.

I use one hand to brace myself on the log behind her, the other wrapped under her ass to hold her up. I drive back and forth inside her, tilting her pelvis until her moans deepen and become louder, telling me that I'm hitting right where she needs me to. "You like that, don't you?"

"Mhmm." She grabs the back of my head and fuses her mouth to mine, digging her fingers in my scalp.

The water splashes and swirls around us as my girl moves faster, widening her thighs to give full access as she twitches, twirls and grinds up and down me.

"That's right baby, dance on that dick. God damn." I eat at her mouth again, savoring her wet clutch around me and the thrumming pulse of the sweet pussy that's only ever felt me, only ever let *my* dick inside. That's a potent thought that does carnal, barbaric things to a man's head, heart, cock... swelling within her to an almost impossible fit, causing the familiar fire of release to start racing up my spine.

When I'm here, in Laney, my wife... all else ceases to exist. My only worry how many times I can make her come before I explode. My only thoughts on how to get closer, deeper, permanently connected to her. My only want to feel her coat me in her, our, pleasure.

"Jesus baby, you..." I lose the thought when she scores her nails down my back to my ass, grabbing both cheeks and

124

dragging me farther, harder, inside her. I slink a hand between us and find her clit, swirling my thumb with the precise pressure and speed I know she likes, till she's wailing into the night, demanding my come from me.

"Whose?" I thrust hard, then ease slowly out till just the tip remains in her moist heat. "Say it. Whose baby are you?"

"Yours Dane, only, always, yours."

That's what I fucking thought.

———————— ⌇ ————————

-*Laney*-

"You look like you just took a plowing," Bennett crudely surmises, with an eyebrow wiggle as we meet her and Zach midway up the resort sidewalk.

"We went swimming," I clip, my head held high.

"Swimming, fucking." She flicks her hand in dismissal, "whichever. Anyway, we were coming to find you to settle a debate for us. The grandparents all went to bed, which means the booze came out, and so did Sawyer's claws. Zach here thinks we should leave it be, that Blaze and/or Ryder, whoever he's targeting at any given second, can take it. I, however, think we should stop him."

"Good God, let's go," I start to rush past her but she latches onto my arm.

"By we, I meant *we* should make Zach and Dane go control their boy while *we* sit out here and catch up. My foot hurts, I need fresh air and I haven't seen you all day."

"Okay, come on." I help her hobble to a nearby patio table and sit down. "Have fun boys! Lemme know if you can't handle it. And Dane?"

"Yes, dear?" He mocks, standing right where I left him with his arms crossed over his chest, brows trying to meet in the middle.

"Remind your son he's not old enough to drink."

"*My* son? First time I've heard you say that in a while."

Zach laughs and claps Dane's shoulder. "That's because she thinks he's doing something wrong. Don't worry, he'll be Mama's boy again tomorrow, when he's sober. Come on. And no wandering off on that foot, B."

"Send someone out here with drinks!" Bennett calls after them. "Alcoholic, made with at least three fruits!"

"So." I dive right in, "where were you all day?" My nose tickles from the suspicious giggle I'm holding in.

"Uh, in my room. Hurt foot, remember?"

"My God, how bad can it be? Is it still attached? Let me see!" I lay my hand over my heart and gasp.

"I do have one good one left, which I *will* cram straight up your ass, ya know."

"Uh huh, nice try on the deflecting." I narrow my eyes.

"If you're choking on something over there Laney, better spit it out." She leans back and folds her arms, glaring at me while pursing her lips.

Here goes… I'm certainly not afraid of Bennett. Over the years, she's mastered "dishing it out." Well, she's about to take it. And who's she foolin'? She asked me to stay out here because this is the very conversation she and I both know she wanted to have, lest she implode from keeping it bottled up.

"What's going on with you and Zachary Taylor Reese?" I grin, leaning in on my elbows.

"I would've known who you meant if you had just said 'Zach.'" She rolls her eyes. "And we're best friends, same as always. Hate to disappoint ya there, Gossip Girl. X-O-X-O, though." She air smooches me.

I slam my hand down on the table. "You are so full of shit, Bennett! I saw the way you treated Tia!"

"Who? Oh, the maid Zach brought snorkeling? Pssh." She flings her hair over her shoulder. "I didn't treat her any kind of way. I actually made friendly conversation, didn't I? And if she can't handle that little taste of my legitimate curiosity, she'd never make it in the Crew. See, saved us all some time and headache."

"And Shane, Mr. Baseball? What's going on with him?"

"No idea, could've already gone home for all I know. And I didn't invite him. Sawyer did," she quips… except a lot bitchier than just a normal quip.

"Did Sawyer invite him *dancing* too? You completely ignored us to bump and grind with him all night."

"Did Zach ask me to dance and I missed it? Didn't think so. I'm in Jamaica, and there was dancing. I danced. No big deal.

Let me ask you this though, did Shane have sex with my face, like Zach and Whorey Housekeeper, and I somehow missed that too?"

She's getting very defensive—Code Red—her cheeks and throat the same color as her hair and a downright evil bite in her bark. Plus, she's now using her hands to talk, and not just any hands, karate chopping the air, or the imitation of a knife slashing someone's throat hands.

Perfect time to push harder. Cause that's what friends are for and all. Plus, I do love myself a heated debate.

"Why's it matter, Bennett?"

"It doesn't!" *As much as I don't want the guys to come back with our drinks and interrupt, this chick could use some calming elixir.*

"Then why are you yelling?" I yell back. She's high on Jamaican air if she thinks I'm gonna sit here and coddle her loud ass.

I can literally see the lumps of control bump along her throat as she swallows down her psycho. "I'm. Not." She *grits* out, but at a reasonable volume now.

"So you're not jealous?" I drum my fingertips on the table, the other hand casually propping up my chin.

"Not at all. Be a little late now anyway." It trailed off in a gloomy muffle, but I heard it.

"*Why?* Bennett, why is it a little late now? *What* is a little late now?" I plead, practically salivating for her to open the floodgates and let me help her paddle safely to the side.

"Zach's great, honestly, he's my best friend in the whole world. No offense, you are too, but you have a family to take care of. Zach and I, well, we only have each other to worry about. Tia just didn't seem right for him, but I shouldn't have been so rude to her. I'll fix it."

Aannnd, we've made a total one-eighty. So fast, I'm dizzy.

"Bennett." I reach over and cover her hand with my own. "You know I want you happy, we all do, whatever that looks like. You and Zach have both brought around a ton of different dates over the years, but this time, this trip, something's different. I can feel it, Ben, just like I know you can too. You know you can talk to me, no judgment."

The agonized noise she lets out can only be described as what sadness sounds like, pure and raw, and it hurts me for her just hearing it. "Zach and I will always be friends, close ones. I'm not going anywhere, and any new bitch that comes slithering around and thinks different can kiss my fabulous ass. But..." She looks off and I see the gleam of tears in her eyes. "Sometimes, when you shut a door, and hide away the key... you forget where you put it, and can never open that same door again."

What does that mean? Did something happen between Zach and her? How long ago? *What's behind the damn door????*

She laughs, although pained and facetious, shaking her head. Guess I said, screamed, either... all that out loud. "Don't over think it, Laney. You're not a locksmith. And I wouldn't call you even if you were. You love your fairytales and happily ever-afters. Well, lemme give ya a big spoiler. Lots of those damsels could've figured a way out of their towers. They didn't *want* to *escape*. They wanted to be rescued."

She stands, all her weight on one foot as she holds out her hand. "Come on, time to call it a night."

I move to take her hand, confused and far from ready for this conversation to be over, when a deep voice startles us both.

"Let me help you, Ben." Zach just inside the shadows, steps forward. I try to read his face, something I've always prided myself at being able to do, but he gives away nothing.

How much had he heard?

And of what he did, does *he* understand all she *didn't* just say?

Part
Two

Chapter 14

Some Kind of Way

Bennett

His set in stone face and blank eyes had the opposite of his desired effect, telling me what I fully suspected. He heard what I said. Laying out the woes of my battered and broken heart in cryptic message that he no doubt decoded. I just couldn't hold it all in another torturous second, so I vented in a way where I offloaded some of the burden, but still felt hidden.

Some secrets can't ever be spoken.

They wouldn't understand, and I'd lose all I have left.

But I can certainly discuss it with Zach.

"Nothing to say? Critique? No follow up questions?" I give him lip as he walks with me back to the room.

His faint chuckle is sharp around the edges. "You drunk?"

"No! Don't you think you would've noticed if I was tossing 'em back?"

"You double up on your pain meds?" He wraps one arm around my waist, stiff and purely for support, probably noticing that my limp's worsening the later it gets, having been on it a lot this evening.

"Just ask me what you really wanna know." Enough with the games and pussy footing around. He holds open the door, waiting for me to enter, but I refuse. I'm not going a damn place until he uses his big-boy voice and asks me an actual question; the one I can smell burning his tongue.

"I just—" His chin lowers to meet his chest, one hand reaching up to scrub the back of his neck. Then all of a sudden, his head pops up. He's decided to go for it. With purpose in his green eyes, he looks straight into mine, nostrils as flared as his pupils. I don't get you, Bennett." He huffs, "What the hell's up with you this trip, huh? Why the bitch treatment to Tia? And the crazy rambling to Laney? Did I do something wrong?"

"No." I exhale slowly defeated and exhausted, so genuine, and shuffle past him through the doorway. "You didn't do a thing wrong. Just ignore me, I'm PMSing." I fib an excuse.

"No you're not." I snap my head back toward him in shock, his cheeks a shade of crimson I've never seen him wear.

"*How* do you know that?"

"You're kidding, right? Bennett, think of all the tampon runs I've made for you, the purple box, *unscented*, cause the perfumed ones are dangerous for, never mind. Or how about all the times I've scrounged up your heating pad cause you had cramps and couldn't remember where you put it. And let's not forget my personal favorite, picking up your birth control prescription for you. That's how I know. Now let's get you to bed before you act any crazier tonight."

Still stunned by the plethora of embarrassing intel he just spouted, I didn't realize he knew *that* much about me, I hobble up to my room with as little of his assistance as possible; feeling crazy enough for it to actually be my time of the month.

I slump down on the sofa and take off my walking brace and *one* shoe, super chic, tossing it across the room. Damn, I was hoping I'd hit something with it. "You know I don't deserve you, don't you?"

"Uh huh," he mumbles, watching me throw my tantrum with amusement tugging at the corners of his mouth, a beautiful mouth, bottom lip much juicer than the top.

"And *you* don't deserve the way I'm acting. So if I was to ask you to stay and watch, say, 'Eagle Eye,'" *I happen to know it's one of his favorites, and I saw it on the Dane-Pay-Per-View list,* "I wouldn't be surprised or blame you if you said no."

"No idea what's gotten into you tonight woman, but you are acting some type of way." He kicks off his shoes and socks... *must be the temptation of Eagle Eye.* "I wanna shower before we start it, though, cause we both know we're falling asleep before it's over. So you want to take one first?" "No, you go ahead, I'm fine."

He reaches behind his head and tugs off his shirt, cause he couldn't have waited until he was in the bathroom to do that just trying to torture me now.

Zach's a big ole' boy, the tallest of all the guys at well over six feet tall, and not an ounce of fat on him. The light scattering of hair on his chest is the same dirty blond as that on his head and the dark tribal ink on both his shoulders is a sinful kind of sexy.

But it's nothing I haven't seen a hundred times before. So why I'm throbbing painfully between my legs tonight, I'm not sure.

"Don't." He says, dark and resolute.

"Don't what?"

"Don't look at me like I *wouldn't* be your biggest regret in the morning. I'm going to take a shower, Bennett. While I'm in there, think about why it isn't an option, and who set that rule. Then cover yourself in head to toe pajamas and get the movie ready."

And with that, he walks to the bathroom and in a few seconds I hear the shower start running. I'm glad he's so immune to the romantic intent and scenery surrounding us everywhere we look. His level-head gives me the self-preserving illusion of *choosing* the reprieve I need to get my own back on straight.

It's just… Zach and I are the staple "single ones" here in paradise, surrounded by half-naked bodies, tangled together more often than not. And all the wedding talk. And though Zach and I spend more time together than most married couples… I'm lonely. Really lonely.

Yes, *that* kind of lonely.

Zach's the only man I've felt safe with, or close to, since I lost Tate. So all those *dates* my friends have watched me bring around over the years? All for show, partly to avoid their pity, but mostly so they wouldn't all start buying me cats. Every single one of those men said goodnight at the door, *if* I didn't meet them on location in my own car, in which case, they said goodnight at my car door.

Except one.

And that *one*, and all the memories attached, is my recurring dose of reality — that no matter how hard I try to fool myself, I don't want to be alone forever.

Would Tate want me to spend out my days alone?

I know without a doubt that he wouldn't. But would he…

Nope, not going there. Enough thinking for one night. I turn off all those thoughts and hobble into the hallway to grab some ice from the machine just in case this throbbing in my foot gets worse.

"Oh, excuse me," I apologize to the woman coming around the corner that I nearly barrel into. Admittedly, I wasn't watching where I was going, but Rahana, according to her resort nametag, was walking backward!

And now that she's gone and no longer blocking my view, I see what had her getting in one last look: Ryder is standing at the drink machine, blushing from ear to ear.

"Friend of yours?" I ask.

"Definitely not." He's adamant. "I'd say she was acting totally inappropriate, but not a lot seems to be considered inappropriate in Jamaica. I didn't encourage her in any way, she's far from my type."

"And what is your type?"

He takes the bucket from my hand and starts filling it with ice for me. "I don't know, I guess… smart girls, motivated and self-assured. The kind who get attention by not looking for attention. If that makes sense."

"Oh, it makes sense." I grin and take the now filled bucket from him. Thank you Ryder, have a good night."

"Yeah, you too."

Call it intuition, or my witchy sixth sense, but on my return, I take a detour bringing me back toward my room up a totally different hallway. And just as I suspected, I see her, but she doesn't see me, far too engrossed. Brynn. Peeking around the corner to watch Ryder, and I suspect, his little interaction just minutes before.

"His type sound like anyone you know?" She jumps three inches off the ground when I ask, surprising her.

Sweet Brynny stares at the floor, fidgeting from one foot to the other as she mumbles. "I don't know, maybe."

"May be, Brynny. Just may be. Night precious girl."

"Night Aunt Ben."

I sneak quietly back in the room, hoping to avoid the lecture I'm positive I'll get if he knows I limped out for my own ice. Thankfully, he's still in the bathroom, so I hurry and change into my sleep tank and shorts set. And just as I'm cueing up the movie, Zach joins me in the living room, wearing only gray gym shorts that cling to his hips, hair damp.

"Where'd the ice come from?" He notices immediately.

"Room service," I smile too big and fib. "Now come watch the movie with me."

Did I mention Zach's a big guy? That means, when he snuggles right up against you on the couch—for the sake of room of course—you *will* wake up at some point in the night to try and escape the furnace that is his body heat.

But even though I'm suffocating, my innards being baked inside my body, I don't dare budge an inch. Because I feel sheltered, feminine, as though this very spot, smashed against this giant, virile man was carved out specifically for me to fill.

"Quit thinking and go back to sleep." His sleepy grumble rustles my hair, draped across his arm that's tucked under my head as a pillow.

We've slept exactly like this so many times, I don't know why I'm suddenly out of sorts, uncomfortable in my own skin. Maybe because the first rays of dawn, sneaking in through the flowing curtains, have brought some sanity back to the witch of last night. "I'm sorry I was rude to your date. I'll apologize." I mutter.

"No you're not and we already discussed this. Stop. Go back to sleep." He tugs me closer to his firm, raging inferno of a chest. "Sleep, B," he whispers a kiss on the top of my head.

No sooner than I'd listened to him, relaxing enough to fall back asleep, I wake again, but this time it's not because I'm roasting alive. No, this wake-up call comes in the form of an incessant banging on the door. And whoever stands on the other side of it better hope like hell they brought back-up, because they just interrupted one of the best dreams I've ever had.

A fantasy so vivid, my heart as involved as my body and imagination, I feel a bit guilty.

Among other things.

"Gotta be Presley." Zach groans, rising to answer it. I already know he's right. Princess P is known for her signature, unmistakable rapid-fire knocking. Kinda like Sheldon Cooper, except she doesn't keep saying your name… cause then she'd remove all doubt it's her, and is probably afraid after so many "cry wolfs," we may not answer.

No, I'm just grumpy this early in the morning. We'll always answer.

"Where's Aunt B?" She's so flustered, she somehow missed me... hiding out on the couch ten feet in front of her.

"You're getting warmer, keep walking forward," I razz... payback for being a dream crusher. "And you'd better be on fire!" Okay, now I'm finished.

"I need your help!" Her hair, so dark it's reflective just like her Mom's, is a tangled mess and the deep, purple bags under her eyes aren't doing her any special favors.

I sit up and pat the cushion beside me, bracing myself for whatever predicament the most precarious of my nieces has now managed to find her way into. This girl is walking, talking proof that the Lord works in mysterious ways, because if she were any more like her father, with whom she shares not one scrap of DNA, they'd be a scientific study somewhere.

But don't *ever*, and I mean never, let Sawyer hear you make a comment of the likes, even meant as a compliment. So much as a hint of an insinuation that Presley isn't one-hundred percent HIS daughter will get you killed. And they will never find your body.

I admit, sometimes I get a hollow, unfulfilled despair deep in my gut, knowing I'll never have kids of my own, *well* past my prime on that front. But then I remember how much my five Squad babies adore their Aunt Bennett, and I'm okay again. There's not one of them whose diaper I didn't change, or babysit multiple times, or take them out for our "just me n them" dates.

Not to mention, I've sat front and center for more sporting events than I can count, and never, not once, did one of their multitude of different teams' colors not look great on me.

I'm such a versatile Auntie.

"Here ya go." Zach returns from the kitchenette and hands me a cup of coffee, one sip confirming he made it just like I like it, double on the cream and sugar, then sits in the armchair.

Oh yeah, he's the male version of me to the kids, the childless, impartial, "cool uncle," so there was never any question that he'd be joining in on this conversation.

"You guys," Presley titters and shakes her head. "So good with advice, unless it applies to the two of you."

"We banging on *your* door at the ass crack of dawn?" Zach calls her out with a flicker of one brow, to which she immediately shakes her head. "That's right, so enough with the sassin'. Now, what's up with *you*, P? No wait, can I guess?"

Her beautiful face blushes, violet eyes doubling in size. "This is probably gonna make me feel worse. If you get it right, that means it's obvious. And if it's obvious, then you're probably not the only one suspicious. But okay." She wrings her hands together. "Let's hear it."

He doesn't miss a beat. "That Ryder kid's taking shit for no reason because he's your beard for Blaze." Zach says with a crooked smile, triumph pulling it up and worry weighing it down. I tap the end of my nose, *ding ding ding*, because he just nailed the answer on the head using less words than even I could have managed.

And as much as I hate to detract from the victory of his Spidey senses in any way, in order for us to be an effective outlet for the kids, I gotta keep him up to date on urban lingo. Can't have him bringing down the "street cred" of our duo.

Especially since Presley's covering her mouth with her hand, so he won't see her laughing… at him.

I lean over and lay a hand on his bicep, *a very nice bicep indeed*, and frown playfully. "It's only called a beard if someone's same-sex oriented and using said 'beard' person to pretend *not* to be same-sex oriented. That applies to *no one* in this little fiasco. Ergo, no beard. But good try." I give him a chin knock to soften the blow. "Presley just knows Daddy would go hella more apeshit over bad boy Blaze than pretty frat boy Ryder. Which he very well may still do. May take him a minute, but your Daddy doesn't miss much." I narrow my gaze at her, "so I'd quit laughing."

Zach blows out a heavy breath, smoothing a hand over his jaw that's decorated deliciously with morning stubble, making an oh-so-sexy scratchy sound. "Shit Presley, what the hell are you thinking?"

"I know," she wails, flinging herself on her back. "Help! Blaze wasn't even supposed to come, but he thinks I'm ashamed of him, it pissed him off, so he showed up! And I'm not ashamed of him, not even a little bit! I'm absolutely crazy about him! But he's not the kinda man who'll wait around for you to let him know you're *with* him, and on the other hand, I *refuse* to ruin Skylar's wedding with my drama. So what do I do now?"

"Um, you missed a key part of the problem," I throw out, then mosey to the bathroom to brush away the horrid combination of morning *and* coffee breath, giving her time to try and figure out what I'm hinting at for herself.

"What do you mean?" She calls after me. *She didn't even try.*

"Think about it," I challenge her and start brushing, letting her ponder a little longer.

"B, please," she whines. "My brain already hurts! Just tell me."

I rinse, and cave. "The more you fake cozying up to Ryder, the closer you come to hurting Brynny."

"*Brynny*? What's she—?" The light bulb finally goes off. "Ohhh," Presley drawls. "Well crap!"

"Jesus." Zach moans, head tilted to the ceiling. "You kids set out to weave a web, you sure do a damn good job. Okay, here's what we're gonna do. Presley, be friendly to Blaze, so he stays pacified. But not *too* friendly, so your father stays as sane as we can hope for from him. And lay off Ryder. No way is Brynn getting hurt in the crossfire of all this bullshit. In the meantime, I'll try to figure out something better. Now go so we can get ready."

"Get ready *to what?*" She snickers.

"Watch it, young lady." He tells her, droll, but resolute.

"I just think it'd be cool to start calling you guys Zennett, or maybe Bach." she laughs.

"Quite the imagination you've got there, P." I try to laugh dismissively, but it comes out choppy and harsh. In other words-fake.

"You're a brat, and no longer my favorite. Now get out." He smacks a big kiss on her cheek before the front door shuts behind her.

I scurry back into the bathroom and lock the door, taking my time to get ready, wondering the entire time… are we really that transparent to everyone but ourselves?

And then I hear the door close for the second time, but this time, it's with a slam.

Chapter 15

Game(s) On

Zach

Our walk down to join everyone else on the beach is made in an uncomfortable, very unfamiliar silence. Ben and I never struggle for easy conversation, until now. She's a few steps in front of me, that delectable ass of hers that's barely covered in lime-green bikini bottoms swaying out a taunting rhythm, my cock taking appreciative notice. I share a bed or couch with the girl all the time; this shouldn't be affecting me as much as it is.

But boy, is it ever.

I thought the two of us were clear on what "we" are, and I had reached a point where I was okay with that. I still date, I still fuck, and I *still* always put our friendship first. Bennett's more important to me than anyone else in the world. But what I'm *not* okay with is being the target for her passive-aggressive, horny-lonely, bait and switch head games. The hot and cold, the *ridicule* in her voice when blowing off Presley's harmless comment, the expression on her face morphing as though the mere thought of an "us" made her nauseous… she knows me too well to think that shit's gonna fly.

Just thinking about it has me so frustrated, that by the time we reach the spot our group's sequestered on the shore, I throw everything I'd been carrying like her damn servant boy on the ground.

"What was that about?" She glowers at me, head and hip both cocked. If she had any idea what her "angry" looked like through my dick's eye… she'd stop doing it. Which is why I don't tell her.

"Don't know what ya mean. It was heavy." I shuck my shirt and sandals, leaving her standing there in all her pissed off beauty as I head for the water.

To find an even bigger shit show.

Since when did the Crew, and its second generation, become so awful at communication? Am I the only one who notices sweet lil' Brynn, our "baby," sitting under a tree, all by herself, *reading*?

I'm well aware that she loves to read, everyone is, seeing as how she's been doing it since she was about five… but I'm pretty sure that can wait until she's not on the beach, on vacation, and maybe twenty feet from the boy she has a crush on.

"Zach attack." JT comes splashing over to my side, the crazed hormones in his eyes flashing like beacons. "Check that out." He nudges me, nodding toward the bridesmaid girl, whatever her name is, bobbing in the water like every young boys' dream. "That Macie, damn. Gonna need to take that Bugatti body for a test drive." He rubs his hands together, grinning like the Devil.

This is the part where I should give him the whole "respect women" speech, verse him on the meaningfulness of a true connection that grows from a slowly built, shatterproof foundation, but he's got a dad for that. Plus, I've got no "lead by example" to offer up. I mean, look at me and my fucked up situation.

But I love the kid and have a vested interested in the kind of man he becomes, so that instinct wins out and I give it the ole' college try anyway. "Just be smart about things, *Jefferson.*" *There, I used his full, real name. That implies superior wisdom, right?* "You have a lot to offer to a young lady, *besides* what you're thinking. Nice and easy buddy. Slow and steady wins the race." I scrub his head and wade away. Best I got for him right now with this weird mood I'm in—several meaningless clichés strung together. *Awesome job I did there.*

"Hey baby girl." I walk over and sit down by Brynn. "Whatcha' reading?" Now *this* one, I can help all day, no matter my mood. I know, I shouldn't play favorites, and I try really hard not to, but Brynn is such an exceptional young woman, exceeding and disproving any and every stigma attached to someone of her age, that I sometimes can't help myself. She's just always held a certain place in my heart, reserved only for her. And much like her Mama, she was born with a soul aged well beyond her years. She's... fascinating, inspiring... bottom line.

"Hey Uncle Zach. Just a romance." She flips it around to show me the cover. And I immediately wish to hell she hadn't. *What the?* I quickly cover her eyes with my hand... seeing as how I'm on such a roll today and this solution somehow makes sense to me, like she somehow missed already seeing the cover *to the book she's reading.* "Brynny, you're killing me, baby girl. You need a good book to read, I can help. Have you ever checked out 'The

Gifts of Jimmy V' or 'When Pride Still Mattered'? Both excellent choices!"

She leans her head on my shoulder and lets out a precious giggle. "You know I have. You read them both to me when I was little. One of the reasons you were in my top favorite babysitters."

"Just makin' sure you remembered." *And hoping you'd want to stop, right this very second, reading whatever the hell that is in your hand and revisit one of them.* I kiss the top of her sweet head. "So Ryder, huh? He's the one who's caught my girl's eye?"

"Oh, my God." she groans, covering her face with both hands. "Does anyone in this whole family know how to keep their mouth shut? No wait, yes, I do! I didn't say anything to anyone, so how do you, I mean, uh, why do you ask?"

Lil' angel, I adore this kid. "Your Aunt Bennett may have had a hunch. Doesn't need anyone to tell her, you know she's attuned to you kids with that freaky sixth sense of hers."

"That she is. Eh, doesn't matter anyway. He hangs out with Judd and Sky's crowd. Older than me, glamorous, grown-up girls that go to all the parties. Ya know?"

"Why do you think your Daddy wanted your Mama so bad?" Her cute lil' face is filled with hope and curiosity as she stares at me, just waiting for me to spout off the golden answer to life. "Because she was *different*, Brynn. She had a natural beauty that radiated off her from the minute she woke up in the morning. She was confident in her own skin, and no one could take that away from her. Didn't hurt that she's as pretty as you are either." I smile, giving her a playful nudge. "You've got something special, Brynn, rare. And the right guy will be able to see it straightaway."

She snorts, also adorable. "What will he see, a quiet nerd in a dirty uniform with freakishly large arm muscles?"

"Do you love to play ball, pitch?"

"You know I do," she answers my question more with the wistfulness in her tone than the actual words.

"Then *that's* what he'll see. That passion, dedication, drive. And being toned isn't a *bad* thing, baby girl." I laugh. "Neither is being smart. And only speaking when you have something to say. Contrary to what most guys your age may think *now*, babbling airheads are far from attractive."

"You have to say all that, you're my family," she mutters.

"I don't *have* to say anything. And being family, I'd also be the first one to be honest with you when needed. Which is exactly what I'm doing, being honest with you. You've got *it* Brynn, and I'm pretty damn happy you think of it as a secret. Lets me know the wrong guys haven't been able to bullshit their way past what you know, deep down, is true, and the right guy's still out there. Now look." I point. "They're setting up a beach volleyball game. Ain't a girl here that can out do you at sports, and I *know* that even *you* know that's no secret! Come on." I stand, reaching down and pulling her to her feet. "Brynny's time to shine!"

"You two in?" JT asks as we walk over.

"Hell yeah we are, Brynn's on my team!" And I'm not just saying that for "the cause," I'd pick her on my team any day; girl's a hella athlete.

"Nice try, old man. It's Crew versus Squad. Me, Judd, Ryder, Blaze, Brynn and Macie against... well, you better find five of the other grand elders brave enough to join you."

"Dane, tell your son I'm about to make him eat sand." Laney comes walking over, rolling her neck in preparation for battle.

"Mama!" JT feigns hurt, hand over his heart.

"Your mama is nowhere on this court, boy." Laney points two fingers from her eyes back at him. "Bring it, *Squad*. Beckett, Evan, get your asses over here! Time to teach these little punks a lesson. Bennett, you make six girl, leggo!" Notice she picked Bennett, *with a hurt foot*, over Whitley or Emmett. And it was the smart choice, as sad as that is.

It's on now. Laney got a whiff of competition and is out for blood... even her own children's. And you gotta love the irony. The most athletic of her three kids, Brynn, stays cool as a cucumber on the mound or in the batter's box. Not a single outward sign of aggression or bloodthirsty competitiveness to be found. Eats Laney's ass every game; priceless.

"We serve," Laney states, snatching the ball from JT's hand.

"*No*, we volley to see who serves," he argues. "You forget the rules?"

"*No*," she mimics him, "we thank our mother for pushing our huge head out of her body and let her team serve."

"I thought *my mother* wasn't out here?" JT zings right back. He definitely inherited her quick wit, and often one ups her; also priceless.

"Oh, he's got jokes. Hope he has next semester's tuition money?" Laney quirks one eyebrow, shit-eating grin spread from ear to ear. "No, nothing else to say? Imagine that. Anyone else have any objections?" She asks the rest of his team, all shaking their heads frantically and backing up. "Great!"

"Emmy, you know I need my warm-up jams! Hit me!" Sawyer hollers to his wife and within seconds, the notorious opening of "Thunderstruck" starts playing right on cue and Beckett's head starts bobbing. "That's the one, Shorty."

"Maybe you should worry less about your warm-up music and more about warming up your old ass muscles," JT goads him through the net.

Well, no one can say we didn't do our job teaching our next generation how to properly smack-talk. See, haven't even started playing yet and the old folks can already claim one victory. Which is going to be the only one we get. Even sadder than our odds? The fact that Laney and Sawyer *actually* think we have a chance.

"Are you sure you don't want to play, love?" Judd asks Sky, sprawled out on her blanket over on the sidelines. "I'll sit out."

She looks at him with half adoration, for always thinking of her first, and half confusion, for thinking there'd be even the slightest chance she'd want to play. Looks like her mama, *doesn't* act like her. "I'm fine right here, but I'll be cheering for you!" She smiles and holds up her phone. "Got our hollaback song ready too!"

And she does, blasting "Stomp" when our song ends.

Dear Lord, let the "friendly" game of volleyball begin. All fun and games till somebody gets spiked in the face with a volleyball. *Those* odds I'd bet on.

Bennett, Dane and Evan are set up in our back row, cause they actually love our children and are able to contain themselves at the thought of competition, but Laney's at the net throwing some sort of gang signs—that no self-respecting gang would *ever* use—at Brynn (who will hand her mom her ass with as much effort as she'd use to take a nap). I'm across from Ryder, just standing here like a normal person, and yep, Sawyer did in fact, just moon Blaze. Which also, of course, means he mooned every *child* on that side of the net.

I'm in the wrong damn row.

Good Stuff. Clean, wholesome family fun.

"Does your family take games this seriously" I ask Ryder.

He laughs uncomfortably. "Um no, not really. At all. We're more about trying to *boost* self-esteem in my family."

Sure, makes sense.

"Okay, let's do this! Come on B!" Laney claps, encouraging Bennett who's serving first for us.

Which would've been great... had the ball have made it over the net, rather than the back of my leg.

A back and forth, poorly directed remake of Game of Thrones ensues, filled with jabs and what has to be considered fouls, both of the vocal and physical variety. I honestly think Sawyer spent more time on their side of the net than ours... but Blaze gave him back all he wanted, I assure you.

By the time they're serving game point to us, shocker, I'm too busy laughing to really play. Bennett has pretty much just stood in place the entire game, not only because her foot's still sore, but because she sucks something awful. Not that we had anyone to replace her with; our choices of Whitley or Emmett weren't just overly tempting.

Luckily, they had a weak link too—Macie—but at least she tried. And she actually helped our team stay within winning distance this long, by providing a distraction for JT, ultimately costing them two players—boy is totally sprung.

But the overall MVP, humble and perhaps unaware, is Brynn. Hands Down.

And when she lands her final serve right where she intended—in front of Bennett, it falls at her feet perfectly, sealing their victory.

"Nice shot, honey!" Laney beams, too proud of her girl to realize she just lost.

Ryder runs over, kicking up sand behind him and picks Brynn up, spinning her in a circle.

I'd eat sand all day to keep that smile on her face.

You go, Brynny.

After the game, I head to my room to get ready for the rehearsal. Not that I have an intricate role in the ceremony, except to support Sky and Judd. Like I always have, and always will.

There's no denying what the two of them have.

For some reason, I pull the gold slider bar over, leaving the door to my room propped open. That ridiculous hope within me that refuses to ever completely die out, the small voice inside my head that's actually convinced I deserve some semblance of being the one, for once, who's pursued, navigating the pathetic move.

I start the water in the shower to let it heat up and find a good playlist on my phone to drown out the silence. "House Party" by good ole' Sam Hunt comes on and well, you just can't *not* smile when that plays. I strip out of my clothes, discovering that half the sand on the beach made it back with me, and step in.

And not to be outdone by any other shower I've taken over the last several years, my hand wraps around my already hard cock this time too. The hot water should ease the ache and tension in my muscles, but it doesn't, only heating my urgency as I tug hard and fast on my dick.

The steam should fog out the visions behind my eyes, squeezed shut, but no, cursed there too. The same image that's been replaying for as long as I can remember is at the ready, front and center, just as vibrant as always. And *those words*, hoarse, unable to be taken back, and *certainly* unforgettable, burn in my ears as I come all over my own hand.

Never goes away.

Nothing, or no one, has ever found a way to even come close to surpassing, or suppressing, it.

Chapter 16

NOT What We Rehearsed

Bennett

There's something unsettling brewing in the air as I walk down to the beach for the rehearsal. Must have something to do with those ancient, urban legends that true redheads, making up less than three percent of the population, are witches. And since I'm a true ginger, I'm definitely picking up on some witchy vibes.

When I stop on the scene, Whitley's shifting people around like mannequins, bossy commands like "stand here, no, not there" firing off her tongue while Pablo attempts to hide behind a tree. And the minister... I'm guessing that's not holy water in his silver flask. Someone really should tell him the sun glints off silver, outing his lil' habit. Not that I can blame him though.

I take a seat beside Laney, watching on in silence, Dane on her other side. You'd think the parents of the bride, ya know, the ones paying for this whole shindig, would be more vocal. But then again, they've both met Whitley.

And wouldn't take this from her for anything in the world.

Oh, make no mistake about it –this wedding is as much about Whit as it is the actual bride.

I know the second he joins us without so much as turning my head, I always do. I can't define it, and constantly remind myself not to try. It just is. But there is one new development... I try not to let it bother me when he chooses to sit by Dane rather than me.

Whatever. He'll get over it, he always does, in the form of some sketch one night stand or another. Surely Tia will be by to clean his room soon.

I try not to let that thought bother me either.

"You excited?" I hold Laney's hand and offer her my biggest smile.

"Yeah," she sighs, although happily. "I know I shouldn't be thinking she's too young, since I was her age when I married Dane." she sniffles. "But *damn* she's young." She laughs at herself.

"Wouldn't matter if she was thirty, or eighty, it'd still be Judd." I offer the truth.

"Absolutely." She nods, firming her bottom lip and straightening her shoulders. "Thanks Ben, I needed reminded of that."

"That's what I'm here for. When you know, you know."

Zach scoffs, from three chairs down, loud enough for me to hear him. Laney gives me an inquisitive look and I shrug just to play it off. I know exactly why he did it, what he's thinking.

"What the hell, Whit? You lose one of your note cards or something?" Sawyer comes stalking down the beach, voice angry and booming. "Seems to be a glitch in your plans, Ms. Planner."

Per usual, nobody knows what the hell he's talking about... until we all look to the front, right where he's heading, and it clicks into place. *Uh oh.* Seems there's been a few last minute alterations made to the procession, Blaze now escorting Presley down the aisle. Which puts Ryder with Macie, although, if judging by the way he's gazing at Brynn, he no more knows he's walking Macie than he does that she's even here. Brynn's her sister's maid of honor though, and JT is of course Judd's best man, so even the incredible Aunt Bennett can't fix that one.

"Presley's walking with Ryder. *That,*—" Sawyer points at Blaze. "—is *not* Ryder. I'm trying to be nice, cooperate for Skylar and Judd's sake, but this shit is not happening!"

And now those witchy vibes I've been feeling are starting to make sense.

Dane stands and goes to Sawyer. "Do *not* ruin my daughter's wedding. It's just a twenty second walk, no big deal. And if Skylar's old enough to get married, Presley's more than old enough to take a quick, *public* stroll with this kid. They flew by themselves to Jamaica, been strutting around in bikinis, and *this* is the part you're worried about?"

"That all it is?" Sawyer asks his daughter pointedly. "Just a change in pairings, for oh," he pops both shoulders, "shits and giggles. Nothing else your old man should be worried about?"

"Stop." Emmett grates, harsher than she's ever said anything in as long as I've known her. "This is Skylar's day. It's not about you, or Presley."

He ignores his wife, glare fixed on Presley. "Asked you a question, P."

"You're still twenty-five years old, right?" Blaze, brave, *stupid, stupid* boy says to Presley and she doesn't even think about acknowledging his question, face turning a sickly shade of mortified.

"The fuck you just say?" Sawyer jolts forward, Dane jumping in his path and Zach out of his chair now too; right in the middle of it.

My eyes find Skylar, head buried in Judd's chest while Whitley and Evan both also try to soothe her.

"Not playing with you, Beckett. My girl's up there crying. Shut the hell up and settle your shit later." Danes whole body is shaking he's so mad, his tone a sinister warning.

Laney's hand is now crushing mine. Like no shit, I think I feel bones cracking. But Dane's handling it (sort of) and I know Laney. She may be dying to go put Sawyer in his place, but she won't undermine Dane's handle on the situation in front of everyone.

But I sure as hell will.

'Sawyer," I duck and dodge the crowd around him till I'm in his face, finger poking his chest. "Why would you do this to Skylar? You know she doesn't deserve this and you'd be mad as hell if some hotheaded, selfish asshole tried ruining Presley's special day. You need to *simmer down!*"

"I agree." He snarls beyond his clenched jaw. "But I don't like being lied to, or tricked, when it comes to my only child. Now, Presley Alexandra Beckett, this can all stop right now, and I'll be able to go hug Sky and beg her to forgive me, if you answer my question. Own whatever you need to, young lady."

I lean around Sawyer to make eye contact with Presley, not exactly sure which message I want to try to convey. Lie to her dad for Sky's sake, possibly pissing off her boyfriend in the process, or tell the truth and literally light the fuse on the bomb?

I watch as Presley looks to Skylar, her best friend, bonded for life, from the start of life... and see Skylar smile, take her friend's back, and nod.

Presley mouths "I'm sorry" to her then turns back to her father with steely determination on her face and a defiant lift to her chin. "Fine, yes. Blaze is my older, tatted, Harley-ridin' boyfriend! Has been for months! And I'm in love with him! Happy?" She screams, throwing her hands in the air.

"Why you lil' mother motherfucker," Sawyer howls, charging toward the not-so-little motherfucker in question.

"Sawyer!" I scream, and catapult myself onto his back, hanging on for dear life. "Have you lost your mind?"

"Have *you*?" He grunts, spinning around, trying to reach behind himself and detach me. "Emmy, Gidget, fuck, I'll even take Whitley. One of you come get your girl!"

"Jesus, Bennett, get off him!" I hear Zach through the mayhem.

"Not until he calms down!" I whack Saw in the back of the head. "And apologizes to everyone, especially Sky!" I whack him again.

How my ears pick it up in all the noise, I haven't the faintest, but I catch Blaze asking Presley, "I thought you said the blond one, Skylar's mom, was the crazy one?" I start laughing so hard I lose my grip on Sawyer.

But the fall on my ass I'm expecting never comes, because Zach's right there to catch me.

"Thank God Judd's a legacy, cause no one in their right mind would ever marry into this family." He shakes his head at my antics.

"Zip it." I snap my hand in *shut 'er down* motion and spin around to lay into Sawyer some more. "Saw, you don't know anything about Blaze, except that he reminds you of yourself! And how is that such a bad thing? I happen to think you're pretty badass. Can't you at least *try* and be objective, give it a chance? Certain things are meant to be, and no one really knows until they try!"

"Can you *hear* yourself when you talk?" Okay, change in the previously scheduled program. Obviously Zach has something else to say. Or shout. Everyone's shocked at his impromptu interruption, even Sawyer, standing perfectly still, *and quiet.* "Bennett Cole, you're a damn hypocrite in severe need of a lesson in 'practice what you preach'! You're—you—God!" He tugs at his hair, face an angry red and incapable of finishing complete thoughts or sentences.

"Don't go anywhere, Blaze!" Sawyer yells over his shoulder, watching the new show. "I'm nowhere near finished with you yet, this is just more interesting. Cause you're a dull fucker!"

"What the hell is happening right now? Did we hire hidden cameras to tape a blooper reel to offset costs or something and you forgot to tell me?" I hear Laney ask behind me.

S.E. Hall

"Sadly, no. We purposely hang out with these people."
Dane answers her. "Please go check on your daughter."

"Right here, Daddy," Skylar pipes right in. "I'm fine, I'll
make Uncle Sawyer feel like crap later. Can't miss this."

Unbelievable. You couldn't make this shit up.

Well, if Skylar's not upset, and obviously enraptured... let
the games begin!

"What the hell are you talking about?" I yell at Zach.
"Come on, you can do better than that! You got somethin' to say,
might as well get it all out!" I wiggle my fingers on both hands,
begging him to bring it. You open the can, I'm gonna make sure
you eat every last bite in it.

When did I become so... hostile? Angry?

"*Give it a chance?*" He parrots my earlier words, sneering.
"Meant to be? Won't know until they try? You are the *last* person
who should be dishing out *that* advice!"

"I give people a chance!" I stomp my foot—*not* the one I
meant to—and it hurts like freakin' hell.

"Yeah, the wrong damn ones. Like Kendall, the complete
asshat, who couldn't find your, uh, never mind." He frowns
apologetically at the kids.

"G-spot?" JT helps him out, earning himself a slap upside
the head from his mother.

"Definitely what he was gonna say." Sawyer grins and fist
bumps JT. "If *you're* having any problems in that area, see me
later."

"Sawyer!" Laney screeches. "Just, no. I can't believe I even
have to tell you that."

160

How have we not been offered our own reality show?

"And cheated on you!" Oh goodie, the theatrics have yet to deter Zach, right back to airing my dirty laundry, in stereo. "But he sure was texting some good stuff, before we were even here twenty-four hours! Why's he back in the picture, thinking the two of you are having dinner next week? Why is his dumb ass not blocked from your phone? And who the fuck thinks being called "sweet tits" is in any way sexy?"

"What? I didn't see that text message. Did you delete it?" Now I'm livid, how dare he announce that sickening nickname that Kendall refuses to quit calling me! Oh, and deleting my texts, yes, definitely that too. I stomp closer, (foot's already throbbing so what the hell), my hand just twitching with the urge to slap him... if I could reach his face. Tall bastard. "And how do you know my pass code?"

He's asking for it with that condescending expression he's aiming at me. "It's. My. Birthday. That's how."

"Her phone code is his birthday? That's a biggie, huh?" Sawyer asks someone behind me.

"Why, Bennett? Why do all the douche bags who I know don't matter to you get chance after chance?" His anger is gone, replaced by a desperate confusion that stabs at my heart.

And I simply can't drum up any gusto with which to reply, only broken, hushed honesty. "Because there's no risk, nothing to worry or think about. Nothing to care about either way. I can't get burned if there's no spark."

"Oh, there's a risk, but not one you realize, or maybe you do, and just don't care about it either. Not enough to acknowledge it anyway. And no spark, huh?" His head slants to one side, the corner of his mouth lifted in pompous mockery. "When's the last time there *was* a spark, Bennett?"

My eyebrows damn near shoot right off my forehead in disbelief. Is he kidding me with this? Here, now, he *finally* asks that? Eludes to what we've ignored *privately* for years, in front of an audience?

"When. Bennett?" He repeats, arms now crossed over his broad chest, his eyes begging me to answer, honestly.

There's no buffering sound of the waves, wind or birds overhead. In fact, I'm pretty sure I can hear every breath taken by our captivated spectators, the only break in the suffocating silence.

"I'm serious, Bennett. Answer the question, right here, right now."

I feel Laney move in behind me, letting me know she's with me, no matter what, hand on my shoulder.

I open my mouth, Zach's eyes lighting up... but I just can't. Instead, I search out Skylar.

"I love you beautiful girl, and this is your time."

And with that, I take off running, on a bum foot, not looking back, hoping our spectacle deterred Sawyer's rampage and the rest of the rehearsal can go off without a hitch.

Chapter 17

The Road to Hell is Paved with the Best of Female Intentions

Zach

I've been having such a stellar day up to this point, I can't possibly fathom it getting any better. And when I feel someone sit down beside me, I'm not just real optimistic this is the big turning point.

Even if the intoxicating smell of lilac, her favorite shampoo, or the imminent spike of adrenaline in my veins wasn't missing, I'd still know instantly it wasn't her joining me. Because she never comes to me.

And I've all but convinced myself that I'm done always going to her. Let her feisty, red-headed ass fight with herself for a change. It's not like I can get a word in edgewise when she's fired up anyway.

I've wandered quite a ways down the shore, so how the hell did anyone find me?

"Cause you're huge, kinda hard to miss, and I'm all cunning and shit, some may even say catlike." Laney answers my apparently spoken question with a snicker and clawing motion with her hands.

"What are you doing here? I figured you'd still be busy kicking Sawyer's ass."

"Nah, he apologized, to everyone except Blaze that is. And there was some serious bribery involved. Saw will be indebted to Skylar on favors and gifts for a long time to come. And we all know Sky will take full advantage."

"Good, he owes it to her. Same as me. I'll catch up with her later and make it right."

"He does, and I know you will. I'm not worried about it and Sky's fine. But at least I understand what's bothering Saw, as over the top as he is about expressing it. What I *don't* understand, is what's going on with you. And a certain beautiful redhead whom I love just as much." Her brows rise up to her hairline, head cocked.

"Laney." I blow out a frustrated breath through my nose and tilt my head back to stare at the sky, hoping the clouds will all get together and spell out the answers for me. "It's already been such a long day, and we still have the bachelor and bachelorette parties tonight, how 'bout we not?"

"Neither one of us are the bachelor or bachelorette, so the show will go on without us even if we're a little late. So how bout' we do?"

If I didn't love her, her persistency would drive me nuts.

"You're stalling," she sing-songs. "Talk."

"I wouldn't even know where to start."

164

"Try the beginning."

Maybe I should. It's been far too long since Laney and I have had one of our good ole' heart to hearts, and if there's anyone who'll give it to me straight, concern for hurt feelings or what I *want* to hear be damned, it's Laney Jo Kendrick.

More than once over the years, one of my own no-holds-barred speeches has brought her down off her high-horse, and she's always seemed to appreciate and benefit from it, so perhaps it's time I signed on for a big dose of my own tough-love therapy.

I take a deep breath and drop my head to now gaze out at the sea—the clouds having failed me—but still not sure what it is I'm looking for. "The beginning is the part that's gonna piss you off the worst, Laney. It'll hurt people too, a lot of people, and I don't wanna do that."

"So instead, you'll just go on hurting, alone? No solution in sight? If you care enough about everyone else to sacrifice your own feelings to protect theirs, is it reasonable to think that just maybe, we all care enough about you to understand?"

She does raise a valid point.

"I get what you're saying, and I appreciate it." I throw my arm around her shoulders and tug her against my side. "But some things, well, a man just doesn't tell. Sorry."

"*And*, you just told me." She smirks.

I feel my brows fold in. "What? I didn't tell you anything."

"Ah," she holds up a finger, "but you did. I know you guys, honorable, respectful, the whole gentleman's code. So when you say there's *some* things a man won't tell, I know the *one* thing you really mean."

"Laney," I grumble, sweating from the inside out, because I did, in fact, just tell her. An innocent slip of the tongue, not considering how savvy this girl is at reading between the lines… but told her nonetheless.

Bennett. Will. Never. Forgive. Me.

Fuck!

"Hey, calm down." She rubs my shoulder. "It's not your fault I'm so darn clever. Quit worrying, my God, I can feel the panic pouring off of you. You really *didn't* tell me, you did nothing wrong. Seriously Zach," she laughs, "did you really think no one suspected you and Bennett have slept together before? Besides, it's no one's business. You're both single, adults, and great choices on either of your parts. What's the big deal?"

"Yeah." I look away, but not too quick, striving for casualty. "I guess you're right."

"Of course I am. But I still don't know why you two were fighting? I mean, I could venture a few guesses, you were pretty clear calling her out on not giving things a chance and some things being meant to be. So, I'm assuming, and correct me if I'm wrong, but you want something serious and Bennett doesn't?"

Elbows propped on my knees, I drop my head in my hands. "Something like that."

"Well, and don't get mad, shoot straight, right?" She asks and I nod. "Maybe she's as confused as you are. You *have* enjoyed *the company* of many a woman who I don't think spent the night at your house to catch a ride to church in the morning. And you damn sure found out whether or not Tia still has her tonsils, right in front of Ben. And the rest of us. Thank you for that by the way."

"I scrounged up the fucking maid at the last minute so I wouldn't look like a tool, sitting there by myself while she was with Shane!"

"And she only agreed to go if you'd dry hump her in front of all of us?" How she literally tells you that you're full of shit in a calm, steady voice, not even saying the actual words, I'll never know.

"I was mad! Bennett needs to make up her damn mind! I was trying to give her a wake-up call!" Now I'm yelling... at the wrong person. "When Bennett needs something, I'm the one she calls. When she's hurt, I take care of her! I'll be damned if pretty boy Baseball swoops in and I sit back and do nothing!"

"You mentioned that before, the other night, how you've taken care of her before. When?"

"Remember that time when she got really sick and just swore it was Swine flu, even though that hysteria had died out long before?"

"Yeah." She catches herself on one hand, about to fall off the log laughing so hard. "Her hypochondriac obsession with the Swine flu was hilarious. I kept waiting," she tries to catch her breath, "for her to give up trying to convince us that's what it was and start looking up symptoms of Bubonic plague or Typhoid fever on Google instead."

"I stayed with her every day, and night. And on one of my many medicine runs, more meds on the list she gave me that *didn't* exist than *did*, I remember stopping in the middle of the aisle and thinking, 'I bet it feels as good to have someone take care of you like this as it does to take care of them.' I must've looked than a crazy person, or a stoner, just standing there, in a daze. Wondering if she was at home, lying in bed, maybe, *just maybe*, thinking the same thing about me."

I hear Laney sniffle and wish I hadn't turned to look at her. Huge tears glide down her cheeks untamed and my guts knot up. Making Laney cry wasn't my intention and is almost more than I can take.

"That's one of the most beautiful things I've ever heard said, by anyone. Let alone a phenomenal human being, about another one just as spectacular." She whimpers, swiping her thumbs under both eyes. "It's one of those things, moments, that'll stick with ya forever. One day long the road, when events and dates are fuzzy, I'll still remember exactly where I was, what I was wearing and how I felt when I heard you say it."

"When'd you turn into such a softie? Hard-ass Laney's nothing but a pile of goo on the inside. Who knew?" I grin, lightening the mood.

"*You're* the one who said it, Romeo. Anyway, go on," she sits up straighter, hanging on the edge of her log for more tales of my woes. If she had a tail, it'd be wagging right now.

"What else is there to say? I lifted her in and out of the tub a dozen times, dressed her, tucked her into bed. Then I'd slide in beside her and hold her close, making sure her body temp never got too hot or too cold. Watched those damn Twilight movies so many times I could probably quote them," I shudder at the memory. "She was on to some marathon about One Tree on a Hill when she got rear-ended that time and was in bed with a stiff neck for a week. It was a little better, at least all the characters were human. Oh!" I snap my fingers, my first real smile since this conversation started. "When she had Lasik done, *I* got to pick what we watched since she couldn't see. Whole Band of Brothers box set, baby!"

"I didn't realize… you really are always there for her." Laney's voice is faint, and she's talking to herself, not me.

"So many nights I held her, after Tate died. Everyone was devastated, just trying to get themselves going, you taking care of Dane. But I took care of Bennett, and it makes me a bastard, I know, but something shifted. I'd lie awake and memorize how she felt in my arms, her soft skin and its sweet scent, the way she'd run her foot up and down my leg when she was dreaming. I knew it was wrong, thinking certain things, but I just couldn't help it. She was so small, and fragile, and it felt so damn good taking care of her. Knowing she needed me and I could be there for her." I glance at Laney, expecting to see the disgust I deserve, but all I find is watery eyes and a sad smile, so I go on.

"I've escorted her to eleven Crew functions where she got all dressed up. Eight of those times, she pulled up her hair and then turned her perfect, milky white back to me and asked me to zip her up. Four of those times, I got every dance of the night with her, and she'd stand on my feet. Have you ever noticed how damn short she is?"

She gives a tiny laugh. "She is pretty darn short. And you, always good at math." She shakes her head in disbelief, it is a bit strange I remember all those details. And for another minute, I think she's totally zoned out, staring at me, but not seeing me… lost in thought. Then her eyes come back to life. "Zach, do you, *love* Bennett?" She asks so soft and solemn, I think she fears my answer as much as I do.

"Very much, but maybe not exactly like you're thinking. Or maybe so." I groan, shoving my hands back through my hair.

"There's nothing I wouldn't do for her, and of anyone I can spend time with, my choice is always her. But I don't think the kind of love I want can exist without total reciprocation. My definition of love requires it not only be returned, but be frenzied, all-consuming and incomparable. And it's not. So I'd have to say, I'm more enamored, invested, fascinated. And I've waited too damn long for what's starting to seem impossible to settle for anything less than everything. But I *could* love her. *God*, could I love her."

She's silent, so I lean forward to see her face, again lined with the tracks of tears.

"Laney, don't cry. I'm fine. And Ben and I aren't really fighting. We're fine, always will be. I promise. And I also promise, I'll always take care of her. No matter what."

"You're so wonderful, *what the hell is wrong with her?*" Oh no, not the reaction I wanted, and certainly don't need. "So, you guys sleep together, get jealous of each other, but she won't commit to you? I'm going to talk to her right now!"

She's on her feet, fire blazing in her eyes, when I grab her elbow to stop her.

"You've got it all wrong. We don't sleep together, Laney. Well, we do, but we don't have sex. That only happened once, a long time ago."

"When?"

"I just told you, a long time ago."

"How long?"

"Laney, just stop. I've already told you more than I should have, and you getting involved or grilling Bennett won't help anything. If you care about me, you'll accept my thank you for letting me vent and drop it. For good."

"Okay," she wisps out, avoiding eye-contact, so I can't say she's lying straight to my face. But she's lying.

She *thinks* it's with the best of intentions and will only be helping, absolving herself of any guilt.

She's so fucking wrong, and I could kick my own ass for falling right into her trap of female trickery to solicit information. *It was the damn tears, works every time!*

I take her chin between my thumb and forefinger and force her to look at me. "I love you, Laney. I love that you care about me, and Ben, so much. But I am begging you. Don't. Help. You don't know what you're dealing with on this one. You'll do more damage than good, trust me."

Green to hazel, our eyes battle in a stand-off, and I see, clear as fucking day... I've got to beat her to Bennett.

Chapter 18

It Too Reads Mama

Bennett

I love my niece Skylar, and had I ever been fortunate enough to have a wedding of my own. Yes, I would've wanted it to be the grand palooza that put all other paloozas to shame.

But damn, how much longer can this thing possibly last? No one's even married yet and I feel like we've been on this island for a month!

Probably shouldn't have gotten here a week early with Whitley. My bad. But a vacation in paradise was too good to pass up.

Now that I've had a chance to cool down and really think about what Zach said, in front of everyone—still not too pleased about that part—all I want to do is go track him down and talk about it privately.

If Zach and I are broken, nothing else works. That'll be it, I will officially give up this farce of survival, I've been pulling off for years made only possible with his help. Zach is my constant, my 'it's not so bad, cause he's here!' I don't *have* to do things alone or force myself through the company of another horrid first date, because Zach will do whatever it is with me. And he'll make it fun. Exemplary. By no means a cardboard cut-out stand in. I *enjoy* my time with him.

But as much as I want to, I can't go to him right now, because I have yet another 'wedding pre-game that lasts forever' event: the bachelorette sleepover.

And if it's important to Skylar, it's important to me. Plus, my presence gives it at least a prayer of being cool. As opposed to the lame as hell it sounds to be on the surface.

"Aunt B is in, let the cool begin!" I announce as I throw open the door with my hands, both holding bottles of champagne, in the air.

"Yay! Come in, come in." Whitley rushes over to me, grabbing the bottles of bubbly. "You can go next to get your hair done!"

"I can what?" I reach up and pat my hair, pretty sure it's already on point.

Laney grunts and I look over at her primped, if that's what we're calling it and bend over laughing. *Oh shit, totally worth it.* When I can talk again, I just have to poke at her. "Nice pigtails, there Rodeo Rosie. You remember to tie up your horse and give him some water?"

"Shut your hole," she growls at me, rolling her eyes in frustration. "Only for my daughter. Now come sit by me." She has that conspiratorial glimmer in her eyes, patting the couch beside her. "Wanna talk to you."

"No wait! Me first!" Sky jumps up and down, clapping. "Where's...?" She looks around the room, taking inventory. "Where's Macie?"

Bet I can guess. I'm tempted to raise my hand and yell 'pick me, pick me' but I think we've had enough shocking discoveries and/or mishaps for one wedding trip.

"I'll go find her," I insist, quick-stepping it to the door. "I forgot my uh, *saddle.*" I grin at Laney." Be right back."

I shimmy down the breezeway that connects all the condos and cut through the middle path, hoping to pull this off caper without anyone seeing me. Do these kids know how lucky they are to have me? They all better hope like hell their parents never get a wild hair and strap me to a polygraph or we'll all be screwed.

I don't know which room Macie's in, so I head straight for his. "Oh, Jefferson," I sing-song as I knock on the door. "Come out, come out, wherever you are! But get dressed first!"

As predicted, there's a shuffle of bodies and feet, and... Macie needs to work on her whispering, before the door opens a crack. JT's head pokes out, complete with sex-hair and swollen lips—good luck hiding that hickey on your neck by the way—and gives me his best innocent smile. "Hey, Aunt Bennett. I was, uh, just getting ready to go meet the guys for the party."

My frown and crossed arms ask him for me, but I say it anyway. "Have you ever felt like you need to lie to me?"

"No ma'am." His head droops.

"You use protection?"

"B!" Now he looks at me, his head shooting up, embarrassment flaming up his neck and face. When I ask again, with one arched brow, he nods.

"Good. Now get your ass to the party before we have yet another controversy at this wedding. You're her brother and that's her friend, Skylar will *not* go easy on you! And you, missy." I push the door open wider and peek around JT thankfully in boxers, to find Macie scrambling into her clothes like the air burns her naked skin. "Let's go! Don't worry, no one will notice your hair, but try to tone down the sex glow thing you got going on."

"B—" JT starts, but I hold up a hand to stop him.

"Nope, never speaking of it again. Not mad at you, still love you, and I know nothing. Got me?"

"Got you." He grins. Macie awkwardly tries to slide past him through the door but he latches onto her arm, leaning in for a kiss.

"No! None of that!" I pull her away from the horndog. "Hurry up JT, go! You, sex kitten, move your ass!"

The poor girl can hardly manage one foot in front of the other as she walks beside me. And the way she's biting her nails has got to hurt. "Hey." I stop and grab her by the shoulder. "I'm not judging you, okay? I just don't want Skylar to have to deal with any more bombshells, okay?"

"Y-yes," she stammers. "I just, it just—"

"Oh, I'm *well* aware it happened." I laugh though strained. "Happened when I was your age too. Now, clear it out of your mind, do *not* get drunk and let it slip, and..." I tap my chin, contemplating. "Say you got your curling iron stuck in your hair and I had to help you. Trust me." I eye her 'fucked do' warily. "They'll buy it."

Her whole body lags with her breath of relief. "I wish you were my aunt."

"Well, keep it up with JT and I just might be one day." I shouldn't have said that, my nephew is horny on wheels, putting the "lay" in playboy. He's funny, smart, looks just like his daddy and comes from money. What'd everyone think was gonna happen? And I'd bet a limb, he won't be settling down anytime soon.

Another crisis adverted, we're mere steps from Skylar's room when I'm grabbed from behind.

"Gotta talk to you." Zach's hot breath rushes over my neck and my skin tightens with a coat of goose bumps.

"Macie, go on in. I'll be in there in a minute," I tell her in what sounds like my sex phone operator voice, cause the hard body pressed up behind me, has my heartbeat accelerating.

Zach drags me around the corner, and I almost miss that fact that he's worried, too busy studying his chest, a broad plane of compact muscles displayed beautifully in his tight gray t-shirt, heaving in and out, speaking sign language to my libido.

Oh, wait, we're still fighting...*down girl*!

"What?" I tame the rasp of my desire in my voice—I tell myself that anyway—and do my best to feign annoyance.

"Okay, don't say anything till I'm done. Promise?" He's holding both my shoulders now, his concerned eyes a deep jade. He can't ever hide it from me when he's troubled, cause happy Zach's eyes are a clear, mist green. And turned-on Zach... I digress.

"Yep." I roll my hand, urging him to spit it out.

"So, Laney came and found me, asked about us, why we were fighting. I didn't tell her anything specifically about that, but she figured it out. You know how she is, fucking mind warps ya before you even know it happened."

I am familiar with the Jedi mind tricks of Laney.

"She doesn't know *when* though, Bennett. I swear. That's why I had to come find ya, cause you know she's gonna talk to you. I didn't want you to assume I told her everything and give her more than she really had. I would never do that to you."

I don't know how or why, but something inside me snaps, and I'm done. Done with the lies of omission, the guilt, and most of all, I'm done putting everyone else before myself. I step into him and run my hands up his torso, leaving one to lay over his drumming heartbeat. "Do you regret it?" I ask, a hitch in my whisper.

Instantly, he answers, husky and impassioned, no room for apology. "Not for a single, fucking second. And I never will. Only a fool would regret perfection."

"Yeah, me either" I agree in eager honesty. "Okay then." I clear my throat and back up a step, acting the resigned, stoic girl I don't feel. "Fuck 'em!"

He teeters back on one heel, caught off guard by my sudden shift in mood. "What?"

"Fuck. Them," I grit out. "Fuck them all. They don't get to judge us and I'm sick of being afraid they will. It's time for us to breathe easily again, quit living under the shadow of shame, when neither of us are ashamed. If she asks, I'm telling her, and you might as well head it off at the pass with Dane."

"You sure?" His smile confirms I'm making the right decision; it's fuller, brighter and more carefree than I've seen in a long time. "So what's this mean for us?"

"I don't know yet. One thing at a time." I shrug. "Haven't even gotten use to this revelation yet. I gotta get in there, and I'm sure they're wondering down at the boys' club where you are. See ya later?"

"Count on it." He taps the end of my nose and turns to go.

Laney still hasn't said a word to me about it and I'm sitting on a hair-trigger, just waiting. But between Whitley's list of games and lots of Champagne, thank God the grandmas skipped this portion of festivities she's been too busy to grill me.

"Everyone, please sit down. I have some gifts I'd like to hand out," Skylar announces, producing intricately put together bags from the closet. I stifle a laugh; if Sky didn't look like Laney, I'd swear there was a mix up at the hospital. The gift bags are pink, everyone's names on them in glitter, with clouds of tissue paper coming out.

But despite the fancy, I know there's tears in everyone's immediate future.

"Macie." She holds out her present, "thank you for being here now, and always, one of my best friends. I love you." Macie opens it, a tee-shirt that reads 'the Bride's Ride or Die Homie,' and a gift card to some store I've never heard of.

"Aunt Emmett." She presents her with a bag. "Thank you for always loving and supporting me, always the calm in our storm. And especially for putting up with Uncle Sawyer. We kinda like him and you're the only woman for the job."

"Amen!" I raise my glass and everyone joins me.

I'm next and my gift is a silk pajama set, same style as Emmett's but in blue to her purple, delivered with an just as endearing of a speech, thanking me for being the one she can tell anything to, earning me a suspicious glance from Laney. *Bonus.*

Presley receives the same pajamas, in pink of course with a pair of earrings and a teary thank you for always being like a sister to her.

Next is Brynn. Her bag is ripping at the edges it's stuffed so full. "My baby sister, the one who is supposed to look up to me, but really, I look up to you, in awe. Thank you, not only for being my maid of honor and best friend in the entire world, but for being my inspiration, the bar on which I set what kind of person I want to be. Yes, you're brilliant, beautiful and one heck of an athlete. But most importantly, you're kind, truly kind. Humble, empathetic, and selfless. I love you so much, Brynny Bear."

Not a dry eye in the room. And just when I thought the hard part was over, and I had no tears left to cry... Skylar asks Laney and Whitley both to stand up together.

I scoot over next to Brynn and grab her hand for strength. If anyone will hold it together for this part, it'll be Brynn. I plan to hide behind her while I blubber.

"Mama." Skylar gets out the one word before she's covering her mouth and sobbing. She waves the other in front of her face until she's able to speak again and continues. "I admire you, the woman you are. You taught me to be independent and strong. Confident. So strong and confident, that you still know how important you are, even when you take a step back." Skylar holds out a necklace and Laney lifts her hair so Sky can put it on her. It's a small silver heart, but only half, with a crooked edge, engraved on it is 'Mama.' "I love you so much. Thank you for being exactly the mom that you are, unconventional and tough, but perfect."

How I can possibly hear what she's saying over my snotty, snorting bawling... no clue. Laney's doing great though, still standing upright, twirling her new necklace adoringly.

"And Whitley. Not that it took a lot of convincing." Skylar giggles faintly. "But Mom and I decided that you would be in complete charge of this wedding. Not only because you'd do a great job, and you deserve it, but because we all know how hard you struggled to have children. I sure am glad Judd's the one God chose to give you though, thank him for it every day. And I know you wanted a daughter too." Skylar is barely understandable now, her nose stopped up from the endless flow of tears, and her hands shake as she holds up the other half of the necklace, "well now you have one." She clasps the half-heart, edges matching Laney's, around Whitley's neck. It too reads 'Mama.' "And you got to plan her wedding. Thank you. For Judd, and for loving me like your own daughter, which I now am. I love you."

That's it, I'm calling it, my heart can't take anymore.

"Oh, my sweet, sweet Skylar." Whitley wraps her new daughter in her arms, soaking her pajama top in tears of pure joy.

After a handful of miscarriages, Whitley finally got her girl.

And Laney looks on happily—for Whitley of course—and because she didn't have to plan a wedding.

Just kidding. Sorta.

I chug my flute of champagne, but a hand stops me from refilling it. "Not so fast, want ya sober for this conversation." Laney simpers.

"Really? Can't we just keep crying, drinking and being happy? Do you think Skylar's night is the best time to do this?" I swat away her hand and pour, generously.

"You just made my point for me, that now's the perfect time. *Everyone's happy*, Bennett, except you and Zach. I can't enjoy all the love around me knowing you're both miserable. Let's see if we can fix that, shall we?"

See, what Laney forgets is, I'm not happy-go-lucky Bennett anymore, who skips behind her, humming a happy tune while she leads. *And* I've been drinking.

And I already gave the green light to set Zach in motion. Time to pull my half of the weight. "Yep, let's do this!"

"Squad girls, stay here, and make noise. Crew women, bedroom with me please, now!" I bellow, and march that way.

Oh sweet baby in a manger... I *did* ask them to make noise so they wouldn't hear, but do we *really* have to listen to 'Watch Me'? Seriously, like four of the nine batters on Brynn's team use it as their walk-up song, makes my brain bleed at this point. But not my baller, Brynn struts up to go yard to "Here Comes The Boom." Hell yes it does.

"Whit!" I snap my fingers in front of her face. "It's *stanky* leg, not *broken* leg, and I need your attention. Ladies, please have a seat."

Laney's nose scrunches up as she sits on the bed... *her daughter* and Judd's mattress of matrimony. Serves her meddling ass right.

"I'm about to tell you all something, that you're not gonna like, because Laney is nosey, shocker, I know, and won't let it go. And because frankly, I'm sick of the monkey on my back." I stand in front of them where they all three sit on the bed—three lil' ducks in a row—and stiffen my shoulders, spreading my stance with pride and authority. "I slept with Zach."

Laney just grins smugly like she knew something first. Let's see how long that lasts. Whitley claps and bounces in place, I'd expect nothing less. And Emmett. Em watches me carefully, her eyes guarded and assessing, her mouth set in a straight, untelling line. She's married to Sawyer, of course she's always waiting for "the other part."

Time to possibly lose the three most important women in my life.

"Once."

Whitley stops clapping, a confused dip to her brow line.

I suck in a deep breath and say the rest on the rush of outgoing air. "Less than a month after Tate died."

There's the gasps of horror I was waiting for.

"I'm sorry. For not telling you sooner," I quickly amend. "And for springing it on you now, of all times." I stare pointedly at Laney. "And I know the timing of when it happened seems like I'm a heartless bitch, you're all well within your rights to think that and hate me, but I'm *not* sorry it happened."

Not sure when I fell to my knees and started crying, but that's exactly how I find myself.

Laney's are the first arms wrapped around me, her tears wetting my hair where her cheek rests. "Nobody hates you or thinks badly of you, Ben. None of us have any idea what it's like to lose our fiancé, so we have no right to judge."

"Exactly," Whitley agrees. "I'm *glad* you had Zach to comfort you, take care of you. Grief comes in many forms, so does coping."

Emmett, with the biggest surprise... *ever*, laughs! Loud and hearty. "The best news is, now that you got that off your chest, you can go back to licking his!"

When my wide, shocked eyes lift to hers, she just shrugs unapologetically. "My husband's Sawyer, hello? Yes, I'm a freak. You and Zach are perfect together, jump back on that girl!"

"Mother, ew! Scarred for life out here!" Presley yells through the door.

Should've noticed the music quit playing.

"Ya'll quit listening or I'm gonna whoop some butts!" Laney's threat is met with a round of unconcerned cackles.

"So we good now, feel better?" Whitley asks me, helping me stand.

"Yeah." I wipe my face. "Thank you, all of you, for being so understanding and supportive. Hopefully Zach gets the same reaction from the guys."

"Whadda' you mean?" Laney gulps, her expression the definition of agony.

"Zach, I told him he might as well fess up too. We're sick of feeling guilty. Why?"

"Bennett, no! Dane, oh God, I mean, that was *his brother.* Oh, this is bad, this is so bad!" Laney's rambling, flinging open the door, scrambling for our shoes, her phone... sanity. "You girls stay here, I mean it. You three." she points at me, Whit and Em, "we gotta fucking go!"

Chapter 19

And *This* is Why We Don't Have More Friends

Zach

I can't recall the last time I saw Dane have more than a drink or two, but he's on number three that I've seen so far tonight… and I was late getting here. But he's laughing and laid-back, especially considering what tomorrow holds; both good signs for me and the upcoming conversation he and I need to have.

The actual ceremony doesn't start until late afternoon tomorrow, so Sawyer and Blaze should have time to recover from their hangovers, which they will undoubtedly have. Yeah, Beckett's drunk and he's bringing Blaze down with him. His arm's actually slung around Blaze's shoulder, need I say more? And the instruction manual he's laying out for the kid is being done pretty good-naturedly, *considering*.

"Okay, one more time, boy. My daughter, your Harley, what's the rule? Sawyer asks him.

"She can't ride with me, *anymore*," he mumbles that last word under his breath but I hear it and laugh inwardly. "Until *you* do, testing out my driving skills and general safety knowledge." Blaze recites.

"Correct." Sawyer pats his shoulder. "Next, slumber parties, what's the policy?"

"Slumber parties don't exist. As far as I'm concerned, Presley doesn't have a bed, or a couch. And if you catch me in either, you will tie me to it and set me on fire. I take her on nice dates then walk her to the door, take a quick peek inside to ensure the perimeter is safe, then take my sorry ass and blue balls home."

"You're doing good, boy, quick learner. You left out back seats and your own bed or couch, but I'm sure you know those are a given. There are no loopholes in this system."

"I got it," Blaze drones.

"Great! Here, have a shot." Saw slides him one, matching him by downing one of his own. Works for me. It's keeping Beckett calm, and has him believing that Blaze, in some unknown realm of possibility, is actually gonna follow these guidelines, he's wasting his breath laying out.

"Judd, let's me and you take on Ryder and Blaze in some pool." JT suggests; perhaps to rescue Blaze, or maybe to save himself from boredom.

"Actually, I kinda wanted to talk to your dad," Ryder tells him. *Shit, unforeseen plot twist. Not tonight, kid, work with me dammit!*

"Please don't," Dane groans. *Yeah, please don't!*

"Man, Kendrick. You're just getting it from all sides you poor bastard. I'm surprised your head hasn't blown right the fuck off yet." Sawyer whoops, slapping a hand down on the table, gut-laughing. "Skylar's getting married tomorrow, JT was late cause he was laying it to that bridesmaid girl and *Ride Her's* about to hit ya up on baby Brynny. You're about to lose your shit, aren't ya?"

"You're an idiot." Evan shakes his head and stands. "You and I are gonna go play pool, or throw darts, maybe find you a muzzle on the way. Get your dumb ass up." He kicks Sawyer's chair.

Still chuckling to himself, Sawyer stands and follows him.

And Dane waits until Evan has him *all* the way across the bar before he turns in his chair to face Ryder. "I'm assuming you haven't changed your mind or forgotten. So, you had something you wanted to discuss with me?"

"Yes, um, sir." Ryder's more nervous than that Duggar kid checking his Facebook feed. "I was wondering—"

Dane interrupts, holding up a hand to stop him, letting out a heavy sigh heard around the world. "I'm in a surprisingly good mood, so I'm gonna stop ya right there and help you out real quick." Dane leans forward, elbows on the table; watching the ice clink around the glass he's rolling back and forth in one hand. "Let me give you a brief run-down of where my head's at, then you can pick your words to me *real* carefully. Sound fair?"

Ryder's Adam's apple bobs with his gulp and he gives a shaky nod.

Dane continues. "The day Skylar was born, I held her in my arms and swore nothing or no one would *ever* take her from me. *Well*, tomorrow, a little boy who spent his whole life calling me 'uncle' is now gonna," he scratches the back of his head, " have to call me something else, because, you see, he'll now be doing just that, taking her from me. Then proceeding to make babies with my first baby. And my son—" He leers at Ryder. "—is so concerned with my sanity, and me keeping it that he decided it'd be a good idea to *lay it* to one of the bridesmaids. Can't tell ya how much I loved hearing that. I'm not stupid, I know he." He stops short and shakes off the rest of the sentence. "Let's just say I don't need to *hear* about it. Which brings me to Brynn, I assume that's whom you wish to discuss?"

Dane pauses to take a drink, pinning Ryder with that special brand of evil eye that only a father can give over the end of his glass. JT shifts in his chair, as do I, cause it's getting damn uncomfortable around here. I can't imagine how Ryder's feeling… but if he goes for it, mans up and goes head to head with Dane he'll have earned at least an ounce of my respect, and may just be worthy of a shot with Brynn.

When Ryder simply nods again, Dane goes on, this time with raw realization in his voice; and I really do feel for the man. "Brynn is my youngest, beloved baby girl, the last one that I have any real Daddy time left with. She's only eighteen, never gives me an ounce of trouble and still hugs me and holds my hand in public. I never have to wonder where she is at night, because if I haven't already checked in with her first, she calls or texts to let me know. And when she accomplishes something big, that she's super proud of, *I'm* still the man she wants to tell first. Brynn's always been too busy with academics, sports and her books she loves so much to worry about boys." He takes a deep breath and damn if I don't do the same. "When Brynn was born, her Nanabug brought her a pink teddy bear that rattles inside when you shake it to the hospital. That bear sits on her bed to this day." He slowly raises his glass and drains what's left of the amber liquid. "Now, what was it you wanted to ask me?"

Can't say I'd blame the kid if he ran out of here like the hounds of Hell were nipping at his heels… cause' Kendrick can give a speech coated with more underlying guilt and insinuation than the slickest of politicians. But if Ryder steps up to the plate—which I'm secretly hoping he does—he's got my vote.

He doesn't run or piss himself. Rather, he sits up straighter and stiffens his posture, clears his throat then looks Dane dead in the eye. "I'd like to ask Brynn if I could come watch her next softball game, and maybe take her to get something to eat afterwards. Would you be alright with that, sir?"

Way to go kid.

Now Kendrick's just gonna screw with him a bit more. His mind's already made up, because. I can see the respect in his eyes, the smile he's trying to fight off. But Daddy's not quite done. He cocks his head to the side, a smug rise to his brow. "If I ask JT, my son, who loves his little sister almost as much as I do, or Judd, who's about to be my son-in-law and not only loves Brynn's sister, but has watched this little girl you're inquiring about grow up her whole life, about your reputation, am I gonna like what they have to say?"

Damn, he packed a lot of intimidating information into one question. I'm tellin' ya, dude should run for president. And no time like the present… candidates for the next election aren't lookin' real promising.

"I don't know, sir. But with all due respect, they're sitting right there," Ryder answers boldly and points at JT and Judd, both speechless and fascinated by the balls on this kid. "Maybe you *should* ask them?"

"Boys?" Dane does just that.

Judd smiles and nods his approval while JT says, "We're all set, Dad. Ryder's good people. I swear."

"Ryder," I bark, and he quickly snaps his head to me. "You're well over eighteen, right?"

"Yes, sir."

"Just reminding ya.' *Because*, that means I can legally kick your ass if you hurt my Brynny in any way. We clear?"

Actually, I'm pretty sure it's illegal to assault someone no matter how old they are… but he gets my point.

"Yes, sir," he repeats, bobbing his head frantically. *He must not know the assault rule. Good.*

Dane chuckles, holding up his hand and waving for another round. "There ya go Ryder, consider yourself warned. But yes, with my blessing, you may ask Brynn out. Good luck I seriously doubt she'll say yes."

Daddy Delusion—she'll say yes.

Sawyer and Blaze are still getting along, drunk and have no idea what they're even saying anymore, but chummy and no one's bleeding nonetheless. Ryder's in the clear to ask Brynn out and I'm actually starting to like the kid. He's only had one beer and is making a conscious effort to get to know Dane a little better. And Dane. He's now *smiling*, having a good time simply for the sake of having one, not just for an obligatory show.

I'm thinking it'd be a shame to bust up such a great night, so I decide to put the little chat I need to have with Dane on hold.

That plan goes to shit the second the girls walk through the door. No one else appears to have spotted them yet, but my stomach's already rolled over and my palms are sweating, because one look at the "four faces of Eve," and I smell trouble. I didn't even have to sniff, it's radiating off them.

Laney's shoulders are cinched up tight by her ears and apprehension is smeared all over her face. Whitley's barely kept tears are glistening just above her bottom lids. Emmett's walking ten steps behind the rest of them, avoiding any and all eye contact.

And Bennett? She might as well have "I dare you to fuck with me" tattooed across her forehead. Google Earth could spot those mutinous daggers in her eyes.

Doesn't take a genius, or even half-ass deducing, to know Bennett told her friends "our news" and one helluva a storm just blew through the door.

"Hey hotties!" Sawyer notices them now and snags Emmett around the waist, pulling her down into his lap, Evan following suit with Whitley. I haven't been counting Evan's drinks, because Evan is even-Steven—never has just one, but never has too many—but the kiss he lays on Whitley tells me he's exceeded his usual intake.

The Allens aren't known for their PDAs. Until right now, that is.

"Baby?" Dane stands up quickly, grabbing Laney by the hips. "Everything okay?"

"F-fine." She does a horrible job of... I think it's supposed to be a smile. "Everything okay here?" She glances at me. Laney's eyes can never hide anything and I see in them what she's asking.

I give a slight shake of my head to let her know, *no, I haven't told him.*

Of course Bennett caught our whole silent conversation as well. "Let's fix that then, shall we?" Bennett bites out, making no secret of the fact that she's pissed. But I don't know why.

'What'd I miss?' I wordlessly ask her, but she ignores me, dismissing the members of the second generation at the table.

"JT, Judd, all you boys go find something to do. Now," she snaps when they don't move fast enough.

Sawyer wants so badly to say something, big mouth open and ready, when Em slaps her hand over it and starts whispering in his ear.

Evan's done mauling Whitley and is now waving over the waitress, because somewhere in between their uncharacteristic dry-hump, Whitley managed to chug his beer... and mine.

And now, Bennett finally answers me. Aloud. "They all know, and were totally fine with it. Supportive, understanding. But *of course,* we had to come running down here to *check on Dane.*"

His name drips off her tongue in mocking disgust, and I frown at her, because it's uncalled for. I get it, Dane is the pseudo-leader of our pack and is no question the one who will overreact about things the rest of us think are no big deal, i.e. the night I took the girls to the bar. But Bennett's out of line this time. He will be well within his rights of reason when this news hits him and he blows up.

And he *will* blow up.

It was his brother.

"Check on me for *what?* They, who, all know *what?*" Dane asks anyone, everyone, his face growing a shade of frustrated red.

Dammit, this is not how I wanted this to happen! Dane was acting chill, enjoying time with his soon to be son-in-law, giving the boy who makes my Brynny smile a chance. And here come these women demanding everything happen right away! I blame technology—cell phones, the internet—no one has any damn patience anymore.

No, I'm giving technology way to much credit. These women could be trapped with The Flintstones and they'd still be busy bodies.

"Ben, I got it." I plead with her as much with my voice as my eyes. "Please. Ya'll go back and enjoy your night with Sky and let Dane enjoy his with Judd."

"What do you got, Zach? Somebody better start speaking English to me real quick." Dane turns to Laney, his tone getting louder and more uneven by the second, true worry, and anger, on his face. "Why are you *again*, traipsing around Jamaica at night? Are my daughters okay? Your mom? What's going on, Laney?" All legitimate questions, as is his mounting agitation.

"Yes, they're all fine, great." She pats his chest, then looks to me for guidance.

And my hand just got forced.

"Dane, let's me and you step outside for a sec." I sigh thickly and move toward the door, glancing back to make sure he's following me. Which he is.

I stop once out on the sidewalk and try to conjure up the right words, of which they are none. I already know what his issue will be, because it'd be my issue too. He won't care I slept with

Bennett, hell, he probably already assumes I'm doing that on the regular. And he won't care on the sole basis, that I didn't tell him; guys don't live by that crazy ass *friends are supposed to tell friends everything* rule the women in our lives seem hell-bent on holding each other to.

No, the only thing that'll matter to him—*and it will fucking matter*—is that I slept with the love of his brother's life less than a month after he died.

I try to think, if it were me, what the other guy could possibly say to stop me from killing him.

I got nothing.

"What is it, Zach?" Dane breaks the tense silence between us and asks me.

"I'm in love with Bennett."

Shit, not what I planned to say at all, not even close really, but it just came rolling out. And now that I've tasted the words, acknowledged them aloud, I know, beyond a sliver of a doubt, they're absolutely true. Whether she feels the same way or not, I'm in love with Bennett Cole.

Well I'll be damned, that feels so good, I don't even care now that I'm about to get punched. Oh yeah… it's coming.

"I know that." He laughs. "Think maybe *you* just figured it out, but I've known for years. Pretty sure we all have. That it?"

"No, man. It's not." I run a hand down my jaw, meeting his eyes dead on, man to man. "I slept with her."

His head falls back this time with his robust laugh. "I pretty much knew that too. What the hell? You've been spending way too much time with the women. It's fine, Zach. Tate's been gone a long time. Bennett deserves to move on, be happy. Should've happened years ago. No worries."

"It did happen years ago." I take in one last, deep breath, and finally say what I really need to. "Dane, I've only slept with Bennett once, and it was just weeks after Tate died."

I'd feel relieved having finally told him, if it weren't for the pained betrayal in his eyes. "I *didn't* know that." His voice is deceptively patient, its calmness more intense than screaming would be.

"I know, and I'm sorry, for the timing, but—"

That's all I get out before my head's snapping to the side, a blinding pain searing up my face. I shake it off though, knew I had it coming, and wipe the corner of my mouth where I can feel blood dripping. "I deserved that. But it wasn't like we set a timer, man. She was hurting, and I took care—"

Fuck. Okay, that one I *wasn't* expecting, came out of nowhere and nailed me right in the eye.

"Quit hitting him!" I hear Bennett scream, and find her, with my good eye, standing on the sidewalk with us now, crying. "It wasn't just him, Dane! I was there too! I needed him, needed to feel close to someone. You know I loved Tate, but you have no idea how I felt. I wasn't even sure! Or how to make it better! But it did, it made it hurt less! You can hate me, but it's true! You wanna hit me too now? I owed Tate more than Zach did. Come on, Dane, hit me!"

"Bennett, go back inside. All of you, this is between me and Dane!" I roar, regretting it instantly because my head's already banging and didn't need the help, but I'm desperate to get Bennett away from here. I do not want her to see this.

And of course, none of them listen to a damn word I say or even *pretend* to be considering leaving like I asked.

Fucking Crew.

Fine, a show for all it is then. "You feel better?" I ask Dane. "We can do this all night, I'm not gonna hit you back. I apologize for what I know seems like really disrespectful timing. I really am sorry about that. And I'm damn sorry about your brother, my friend, and Bennett's fiancé."

This time his punch just barely grazes my chin because Beckett catches his arm from behind. "Enough, Kendrick. You don't keep hitting a man who's not fighting back. I get you're mad, hurt, whatever. But punching Zach won't bring Tate back and it won't undo what's done."

"I thought you were drunk there, Obi?" Evan asks. "I'm impressed."

"Watching one of your best friends beat the shit out of one of your other ones has a way of sobering ya up. Waste of damn good tequila too, fuckheads. Now…" Beckett looks at Dane, then me. "We done here?"

"Dane?" I ask him. I'll stand here all night and take his licks if it helps him process, and hopefully, forgive Bennett and I.

"I'm not sure." He says, his tone sullen.

"Hey, hi, quick question." JT steps through the crowd. *Yeah, the Squad doesn't listen to what they're told any better than The Crew.* "First of all, nice arm there, Daddy-O. And Uncle Zach, Skylar is gonna be *pumped* that you have shiner in her wedding pics. But seriously, Dad," he looks at his father, "would Uncle Tate want Bennett to be alone, lonely?"

"No." Dane stares at the ground and shakes his head, "no he wouldn't."

"And if it's Zach who prevents that, would he approve? Of Uncle Zach in general, I mean." Laney steps up behind her son and wraps her arms around him. "Would he have any concerns about the kind of man he is, or that he'd be good to Aunt B?"

"Answer our son, Dane." Laney says.

Dane lifts his head and meets my eyes. "He'd definitely trust Bennett to Zach. Might have hand-picked him, truth be told." He steps forward and extends his hand. "I'm sorry. I shouldn't have punched you. Three times. But, he *was* my brother. Surely you can understand that and accept my apology. And even if you don't, I hope you don't let this keep you from pursuing whatever it is you want with Bennett. Or she wants with you. I just, it caught me off guard, ya know?"

I shake his hand and pull him in for one of those man-hug-back pat things and talk low so only he can hear me. "S'all good, you hit like a five-year-old little girl."

"Tell that to your black eye, fucker." He laughs.

"Does *anyone*, have *anything* else they'd like to announce? Confess? Declare? Speak now, or please, for the love of all that's holy, forever hold your peace!" Evan says. *Yep, definitely drank more than his usual.*

"I bought JT his first box of condoms!" Sawyer proudly proclaims.

Fucking Beckett.

"Oh, and Judd too! Actually, it was one trip, the three of us, so it really only counts as one thing." He just *had* to add in there.

"Quit. Talking." Evan shoves Sawyer while JT and Judd slink away. "Thinking Dane's all punched out, but I'm willing to take a swing at your mouthy ass."

"Great." Bennett claps, once, sharp and loud. "Thank Christ the wedding's tomorrow. Much more of all this fucking fun and we might not survive. I vote we call it a night."

Everyone agrees with her and Evan walks back inside, holding Whit's hand, to pay the tab.

"Dane, you're sharing a cab with me, as in, *just you and me*. Let's go, Rocky!" Bennett grabs his arm and drags him away before he can protest.

No idea what that's about… and I'm praying like hell no one ever tells me.

Chapter 20

Supposed To Be You

Bennett

Dane and I had quite the cab ride back together. We both got out a lot that needed to be said, and I think we understand each other better now. Most importantly, I explained how, of all people, I was able to forgive myself of any guilt. With as few details as possible, I made it clear to Dane that we weren't talking about some animalistic night where I forgot all about Tate and just went at it with Zach. It was honestly a reprieve from the pain, where nothing else existed—or ached—and I was able to feel at peace, comforted for a while.

That seemed to make him feel better. I'm pretty sure he was imagining something else in his mind.

And he's *crystal* clear on one other thing too now: he ever hits Zach again and I'm coming for him. He won't know how, or when, but one day he'll turn around and boom, there I'll be, Bobbitt blade in hand, aimed at revenge.

I was there, in that bed with Zach—*trust me, I remember*—half of the equation, but no one punched me. And Zach just stood

199

there and took it. Fighting back was never even an option that crossed his mind. And let's face it, everyone knows that all six-foot-four, two-hundred and forty pounds of Zachary Taylor Reece could throttle Dane if he was so inclined.

The *only* man I know who'd even have a prayer against Zach is Sawyer. And that shit would be worthy of someone buying it on Pay-Per-View and throwing a watch party. I'd bring the chips, and bet on Zach.

"So you and I are good?" I ask him one final time. He *did* buy me the house I live in, the one Tate had picked out for us, and he also handed me Tate's gym, free and clear. I wouldn't feel right about keeping either if Dane wasn't truly okay with things, or me.

He may be a bossy, overreacting pain in my ass, who puts the capital "A" in alpha (and the "ass" in *pain in mine*, as I mentioned)—but I love him dearly—and as much defiant "don't give a damn" as I try to exude… I *do* give a damn. I couldn't live with myself if I knew Dane thought badly of me.

"Always, Bennett. And if things don't work out with Zach, or even if they do, Laney and I are always right here for anything you need. That will never, ever change. Love you." He kisses my forehead. "Now go find your boy and tend to his wounds."

We part ways with a final hug and I beeline it to the door of the only person in the whole world that I *really* want to talk to right now.

But when I get there, fist up and ready to knock, something sudden and indefinable stops me. I stand there mulling over what I want to say, what result it is I'm hoping for, and finally acknowledge… I don't know.

But I *do* know I can't just sleep on it, all the questions, doubts, hopes, and desires swirling around inside me like an anxious, yet fearful whirlpool.

So I do what any coward would do, I sit down right in front of his door, lay my forehead against the wood, and start to talk to myself, releasing all the turmoil I've carried inside for too long into the atmosphere.

Completely nuts? Perhaps. But it's a much-needed outlet, and Zach won't hear me, most likely in bed with a bag of ice on his face. Win-win.

Let the big, bad universe figure out what to do with it all, because frankly, I'm exhausted.

"I'm sorry about your face," I begin in a lulled tone. "No one should ever mess with that gorgeousness, but I'm so proud of you for not hitting him back. You're all a man should be Zach Reece. Restrained intensity, quiet force and a gentle soul. I'd be utterly lost without you, just in case you didn't already know that. And I know I don't thank you or tell you how important you are to me, the most intricate part of my life really, near often enough. You do so much for me and never ask for anything in return. You think I don't know how many dates you've cancelled or bailed on early to come to my rescue? Not gonna lie, I clogged my sink on purpose to pull you away from that Ann or Annie chick, what the hell ever, she was ratchet." I laugh, swiping a few stray tears off my cheeks. Then I reposition, because this floor is hard and unforgiving, turning to lean my back on the door now, knees pulled up to my chest.

"I hate when you go on dates. No, I *loathe* it, to the point of wanting to break something, or someone. I always wonder, 'is he laughing as much with her as he does with me? Does she act all pissy when he eats off her plate? Do you feel comfortable enough *to* eat off her plate?' Cause you damn sure do mine. I don't even *like* green beans, Zach. I order them for you. Then I think, 'she better not even think about reprogramming the buttons on his radio, I worked hard getting those exactly how we like them. One through three is *me*, four through six all you. And bitch is going to bleed if she readjusts the position of the passenger seat, took me forever to get it where I can see out the windshield without stretching.' But most of all, I feel physically ill, a pain so bone-deep it almost cripples me, when your sheets or shirt, still linger with the smell of sex. Or perfume. Or sex with a skank who wears cheap perfume. Not that I can fault you for it, but I don't like it. I fucking hate it. Did you know I haven't been with anyone since you?" I laugh again, but it's sharp and filled with bitter resentment. And a pinch of pathetic. "Nope, no one. *Years, double-digits*, and not a single one. I have a punch-card for the sex toy store, one of those buy ten, get one free things. I've gotten, hmmm, I'd say at least twenty free *items*. Unfortunately, I'm not exaggerating."

I literally just heard the universe laugh at me. Eh, at least it's listening.

"So many times I've wanted to just grab your face and kiss the hell out of you, or straddle your lap and rip your shirt right off your body. Maybe sneak a hand under the covers when we're lying together. Answer the door to you naked. Something, anything! But I'm afraid, *terrified*, to lose my best friend. That whole friends with benefits thing *never* works out in real life. It either ruins the friendship, which I'll clit-flick myself until my hand falls off before I risk that, *or* the two people end up together, some big epiphany suddenly hitting them that they were meant to be together. And I know that's not an option with you. Figured if you hadn't made a move in the last decade, you probably weren't going to. You don't do serious relationships, I know this. I mean, look how old we are and you've never lived with a woman, been engaged, hell, your longest relationship was four months and twelve days. Yes, I counted. She was nasty too, by the way. *Ivana.*" I snort. "Please, she wasn't a damn Trump!"

"*I vanna kick her ass*, is more like it."

"Ma'am, can I help you?"

I startle, so caught up in my tell-all that I didn't even notice the housekeeper—*not Tia*—stop in front of me.

"Actually, yes. You got a pillow on that cart?"

"A pillow?" She thinks I'm insane, her puzzled expression all but screams it. "Would it be better if I helped you get a replacement key card?"

"Nope, just the pillow please."

"*Okaaay.*" She drags it out, producing a pillow from the bottom of her cart and handing it over hesitantly, like it's a live bomb, or again, like I'm insane and may suffocate myself with it. "You, have yourself a nice evening, ma'am."

"Will do." *No I won't.* "Thank you."

Ah, much better I lay down, nice and comfy, in the middle of the concrete breezeway cause' that's how I roll... and try to remember where I left off in my autobiography.

"As I was saying, I won't lose you or ruin what we have for an occasional tumble between the sheets. And I'm not gonna do it with anyone else, because at this point, not only has my vagina probably closed in on itself, but... once you've had scorching, you can't go back to lukewarm. *Yes*, it was scorching, but also tender, and loving. I'd rather keep what we had together as my last memory than risk some other sub-par excuse for companionship clouding the image. And—"

Wait just a damn minute...

Oh my God, that's it! That's what it's been this whole time! The harsh twinge in my chest turns to a steady, hollow suffering from the enormity of the realization I've just come to. Capable tears pour down my face and I sit up, wrapping my arms around myself.

Everyone always says the people in Heaven are looking down on you. Does that mean they can see *everything*? Even your thoughts?

I sure hope not.

But I've come too far now to deny myself the liberation this piteous little chat I'm having with myself is actually bringing. And I'm on the fence about the whole "see your thoughts" thing, so I might as well say it out loud.

"I loved Tate with all my heart, and I would've been happily, madly in love with him, for the rest of my life. That was the plan. And now I know why I've felt so guilty all these years, and never dared to dream for an us, Zach." I swallow hard, the shame not going down easily. "Maybe it's because we were so young, or maybe that's just an excuse, I don't know. But Tate and I... well, it wasn't like us. He and I, we weren't... you and I are closer. There's a deeper level there that's hard to explain and even harder to admit. I feel absolutely terrible saying this, but it's true. You and me, we talk about things Tate and I never did. You notice everything, the little things that he, didn't. And being *together*—"

I go back in my mind, pulling from the deepest recesses any and every memory I can of Tate and I; how it felt, what *I* felt... and stop. It's too much.

I stand up and grab the pillow, hugging it to myself.

"I think that's enough for now. I know you didn't hear a word I said, and that's okay, I needed to do this for me. God knows best, Zach. It took me until just now to fully come to terms with that. I'll never speak of this ever again, but," deep breath, "It's supposed to be you."

I turn and walk away, steps weighted by my conundrum, feeling both lighter and heavier than they, I, ever have in my life.

As I open the door to my room, my phone dings with a text. I pull it out of my pocket and sway on my feet when I read what it says.

Zach: It IS me, Ben.

Chapter 21

Cat and Mouse

Zach

I don't claim to know a damn thing about weddings, but I'm starting to suspect there may have been some validity to all of Laney's complaints about paying for a wedding package—that doesn't come in a package.

It's almost time for the ceremony to start and I haven't seen or been able to get ahold of Bennett all day. But I've seen Pablo—twice! Now why is it I can't turn a corner without running into his ugly ass, but I can't find my gorgeous lil' redhead anywhere?

It's because, according to Evan, the girls started prepping at the crack of dawn. Hair, make-up, bridal luncheon and whatever else he listed after I quit listening. Surely Bennett can do her own hair and make-up, right? Right, I've actually seen her do it! Many times. But no, my logic's apparently illogical on this point too, because I've also been informed that Skylar insisted all the women, grandmas too, all get the full works done together.

Killin' me.

Last night, it took every ounce of willpower in my body not to jerk open the door and wrap Bennett in my arms, then wrap our bodies around each others'.

But, as much as my dick hates me for it today, that wasn't what Bennett *needed* from me most right then. And that's what I do, gladly; I put Bennett's needs before my own. She'd been carrying around the burden of all that she unloaded last night for years. There was no way I was going to interrupt her and deny her that release, or possibly embarrass her.

And somewhat selfishly, I *wanted* to hear it. Her complete honestly, unrehearsed or refined, the things she'd never say if she knew I was listening. Things I've spent years wondering about, second-guessing myself on and holding myself back from asking her about or pressing her for more on for way too damn long.

Now I know.

And fuck me if it didn't feel fantastic to hear it.

But now that I can finally assure her that her every fear is mirrored by my own and I'm still more than ready to jump, take the risk, only with her, I can't fucking find her!

Drivin' me out of my mind.

I jump up at the knock on my door, ravenous for the emerald-eyed redhead I just know is waiting on the other side. I can't even begin to imagine the look on my face when I open it to find Dane standing there.

"*Shit.*" He winces. "Sorry about the eye, man." His expression is one of regret, but his mouth, twitching at the corner, is totally saying *nailed the son of a bitch!*

"Uh huh, eat a dick, Kendrick." I grumble and step back to let him in my room.

"I'm gonna go ahead and pass, but thanks. Here, I brought your outfit. Where the hell do you find clothes to fit your big ass?" He laughs.

"Your wife. She picks 'em out then delivers them to me, naked." Huh, no laugh from him on that one. Go figure. "And why exactly do I need an outfit? I brought clothes, you've seen me wear them."

"Sky wants us all wearing the same thing. Beach wedding, beach attire." He shrugs, happy to do his daughter's bidding.

I don't even wanna think about the hoops we're all gonna have to jump through when Presley gets married. She's ten times the princess pants that Skylar is. Not to mention, she's an only child and the whole damn apple orchard of Sawyer's eye. He told me once, drunk, (and not gonna sugar-coat it, a lil' sappy), that the reason him and Emmett never had any more kids is because he didn't want to risk Presley ever doubting his love for her or the fact she is *his* daughter; like one child being biologically his might cause her some insecurity. He just wasn't willing to take the chance.

So imagine what he'll see to it she gets for her big day.

"I get that the groomsmen all need to match, but the rest of us too?"

"Just put on the damn outfit, One-Eyed Willie. Jesus, you're whining about it worse than Beckett." He chuckles on his way out the door.

I survey the situation—okay, not as bad as I thought— khaki shorts and a white dress shirt. Preppy beach boy—has

Skylar written all over it. But I won't be surprised if Judd shows up in his Wranglers and boots, despite what his bride says.

When I walk down to the beach where the nuptials are taking place, I *finally* lay eyes on that familiar, flowing mane of russet hair, and the tightness I've been toting around in my chest all days slackens. Just from seeing her, if only the back of her head. Clever lil' witch has purposely already taken her seat, wedging herself protectively between Laney's mom and Emmett. She knows that will stop me from demanding we talk right now, but it's merely a road bump, that *won't* slow me down for long. I smile to myself; this little ploy of hers confirms that her thoughts have been centered around us all day too, so much so, that she'd strategically placed herself before I got down here, probably rushing to that exact spot.

Enjoy it while you can Bennett, I'm coming for ya.

Everyone else starts taking their seats. What the hell, I don't even know who half these people are. Is wandering up to weddings to which you weren't invited and know no one at some sort of Jamaica thing or part of the package? Random seat-fillers included. Just as I pick a chair, beside Evan's dad, someone I actually recognize, the music starts. Judd steps up next to the minister in the front, coincidentally enough… wearing the same thing as I am. *Women.*

All heads turn to watch as two by two, the wedding party makes their way down the sandy aisle.

Except mine.

I'm staring at Bennett, as breathtaking as I've ever seen her look. Shoulders bared by the strapless mint green dress she's wearing, held in place by her perfect breasts and stopping in the middle of her flawless thighs.

And she knows I'm looking. Stealing quick glimpses my way out of the corner of one eye, her chest, where my own gaze keeps returning, moving up and down quickly with her accelerated breathing.

Good thing we were "instructed" to wear our shirts untucked, cause the sight of her has me hard. And the draw, the game of cat and mouse, testing each other, seeing exactly how long we can withstand temptation, thrive on anticipation... can't say I'm not enjoying it. Because I know this particular game will soon be coming to an end, and a whole new round, with endless possibilities and much bigger prizes begins.

The big moment finally arrives, and when Dane's asked to give Skylar away, I pivot my attention back that direction. I don't want to miss this part, because in a way, we're all giving her away, to Judd, expanding our coveted circle. No, strike that, we're not giving anyone away. We're circling around the new, smaller ring being built inside our own. And inside it, they'll be safe, because we've spent years strengthening that outer circle, forged from the hardest, unbreakable steel.

When Dane turns to take his seat beside Laney in the front row, I swear I see the shine of tears in his eyes.

Don't blame him a damn bit.

Who'd have thought it... Laney's (also Dane's but irrelevant to my point) daughter is marrying Evan's (also Whitley's, but again, stay with me here) son. I can't possibly be the only one who catches the irony in that. But anyone looking at

Judd's face right now, and obvious depiction of how much he truly adores Skylar, could never deny—no matter how they got here or where they came from—they were born to be together.

After Judd gets his kiss and seals the deal, we all stand and applaud the newlyweds. And as the crowd, yes, the strangers too, begin to move and make their way to the reception tent, I lose sight of Bennett in the shuffle.

But catch up with her quicker than I'm guessing she'd like for me to.

"You avoiding me?" I move in on her from behind, brushing her hair aside to ask it on a whisper, mouth at her temple. I take egotistical thrill in the goose bumps I see dot her flesh in my wake.

"No," she says in a small voice, leaning ever so slightly back against me, perhaps as starved for contact with me as well. "Busy day is all."

"You look beautiful, Ben."

"Thank you. You look pretty handsome yourself. I have to go though, see if Whitley or Laney need help with anything."

She starts to move away but I slide an arm around her tiny waist and hold her captive. "You shouldn't be on your foot so much. They've got it handled, come sit with me. Let's talk."

"My foot is fine," she says defensively and I can sense her putting up that protective shield of hers as fast as she can. "I need to at least offer to help."

"Fine, you do that, I can wait. But I swear to God, Bennett. You go back to icing me out after that hallway confessional of yours and I might very well lose it."

She sucks in a sharp hiss, as if offended. "I can't believe you're bringing that up! And I'm not icing anything, there's just things that need to be done. Now go find our table and I'll be there in a bit. It's almost time for the toasts, dances and stuff."

"Whatever you say," I growl, letting my tongue tease the shell of her ear. "But be clear, I won't wait all night." I slide my arm off her, reluctantly, ensuring the touch lingers, and set her free.

I don't know why I'm even surprised; girl's her own worst enemy. Walls come down, so you get a peek at the real Bennett on the other side, then go right back up, twice as fast constructed with double the bricks. Discouraged but not deterred, I take my appointed seat at Table Four and grab the card across from me with her name on it and put it at the spot right the fuck beside me. I recline in my chair, one arm draped across the back, and watch Bennett, up, running around, trying her best to look busy, so I decide to partake of this elusive package I keep hearing about and grab a drink every time a waiter passes by. Emmett and Sawyer come join me at the table, rescuing me from sitting by myself like a complete tool, and Sawyer follows my lead on the drink swiping.

I give a small, encouraging smile in all the right places as Brynn gives her toast to the new couple. Then Laney stands and gives her own speech, like only Laney Jo can; witty, meaningful and quick to the point. I'm proud of her, she made it all the way to the end without breaking down, like a champ.

But the showstopper is JT's toast, not only to his older sister, but his life-long best friend.

"If I could have your attention, it's time for me to give my best man speech. Don't worry, it's wicked good. I looked this shi—uh, stuff, up, and traditionally, the maid of honor relates her toast more toward the bride and mine's supposed to be for the groom. Well rip up your programs people, cause that's not how I'm doing it. You see, when you come from an honorary family who does everything with each other, even marry, but not the whole inbred thing, we haven't crossed over to that yet." He laughs along with the audience. "There's no way I can speak to one of them more than the other. Because just about every memory I have of Skylar, my big sister, has Judd in it too. And Judd's been my best friend since before we could speak full, legible sentences that the other one understood, and guess what, Skylar was right there then too. So anyway," he says, looking at them, "this is for you both."

A screen slides down behind the main table right on cue.

"Ah, phones with cameras, greatest invention ever, and shout-out to the parents who give you one when you're young." JT laughs. "And I'm a hella photographer, ready at all the right times, if I do say so myself." He clicks the remote in his hand and the first image pops up for us all to see. "This would be Judd, not a real doctor, repairing Skylar's knee when she crashed her bike. I took this shot with every intention of blackmailing her later, because we weren't allowed to ride down the huge hill on Oak Street. Which is one of the main reasons we did it of course. But, Sky took too long to give me anything to blackmail her on and I eventually forgot I had it." We all laugh now, even Dane.

JT clicks the remote again. "This one's a classic! What we have here folks, is my sister and best friend hiding behind the pool house. This award-winning shot was snapped only seconds after what I *believe* was their first kiss. Am I right?"

Skylar glares at him, but Judd nods his head while wearing a huge grin.

The pictures go on for a while, with a description from JT for each. It's a love story, a timeline of their amazing journey together, captured forever. Thanks to one nosey little brother; which I'm sure Sky appreciates now... not many people have a picture of every cherished memory. Multiple Halloweens, Judd always the prince to Sky's princess. Skylar scrunching up her nose as the first bass she ever caught dangles from the end of her pink pole, Judd smiling at her side. Skylar in her cheerleader uniform, cheering on the sidelines as Judd ran in a touchdown. Judd holding up a big sign asking her to prom. And the best, which earned a round of laughter from everyone except the four parents, who wanted to smile, I know they did... Judd climbing the trellis to Sky's window.

"And this." JT's voice softens to a pitch I've never heard him use and he appears to be a bit choked up, "this is Skylar sitting in her bay window a few hours after you asked her to marry you. I think it may be my favorite. You make her happy, Judd. You always have. Whenever none of us could talk her out of crying, or make her see reason, I'd call you... and no sooner than you got there, she was right as rain again. All she ever needed was that reminder that she always had you, no matter what or against who, on her side. Most guys would've been pissed when their best friend made a play for their sister, but I never did, because I knew that's not what happened. You didn't make a move, the two of you met in the middle. And of anyone, I'm glad it's you, bud. Doesn't mean I won't still kill him if ever needed Sky. You have my number." Like his father, he flashes his sister a wink. "So congrats." He raises his glass and we all do the same, "to Judd and Skylar, two of my favorite people in the world. Keep being happy, you sure know how."

Damn fine speech, again, so much like his father. Everyone's now on their feet clapping, overcome.

Dinner is then served, still no Bennett at the table, and I manage to choke down the plate of chicken a-la something, that I don't remember ordering. On any other night, when I wasn't sitting on impatient pin and needles, it probably would've tasted pretty damn good. *Guess Ben's not hungry? Or not ready to face me yet?*

"And now, it's time for Mr. and Mrs. Judd Allen to have their first dance as husband and wife." Oh look, turns out Pablo did have at least one specific task and managed to pull it off: that announcement. Just as Skylar and Judd make their way, hand in hand, to the dance floor, Bennett slides into her seat beside me.

"Fancy meetin' you here." I lean into her and tease, low and smooth.

She laughs, such a melodic sound. "Why Mr. Reece, have you been partaking of the free champagne?"

"Guilty." I nip her ear, but she brushes me away and shushes me with a stern frown.

"The first dance is a big deal, pay attention!" Her scold is hushed, but she definitely expects me to listen to it.

Hey, I know this song they're dancing to! *How* do I know this song they're dancing to? "Turning Page," she says softly, running her hand down my arm. "It's from those Twilight movies I made you sit through." And the warm, full-on smile I've been waiting for her to grant me all night appears as her foot finds my leg under the table.

"You didn't make me do anything." I lay my hand over her knee and rub gently. She tenses, but she'll just have to deal; I can't go another minute without touching her. It's absolute torture being close enough to smell the sweet scent of Lilac that always seems to linger on her skin, hear her voice and laugh… yet still feeling miles apart from her. This subtle physical contact at least narrows the gap, that's all day seemed insurmountable, so I can keep my cool until the party's over and I can finally get her alone. "I'd watch whatever you wanted, Ben. Anytime."

Everything turned out beautiful; Whitley has once again outdone herself. Pablo better be glad he had her. You couldn't have asked for a more idyllic wedding; the warm air, delicate breeze blowing in off the water and a white tent filled with the easy glow of candles.

There are certain "big" moments at a wedding where it's expected and respectful to actually pay attention… especially if you're Aunt to both the bride and groom. Which is why I force myself to brush Zach's hand off my knee and scoot my chair a bit away from him.

I can't do this with him now. The ambience of the wedding is already confusing me enough, filling my head with a romantic, whimsical haze. I can't handle him touching me too! He looks so damn sexy, dark blond hair styled like he didn't even try, his white dress shirt opened just enough at the collar for me to sneak a peek at the ripped chest that lies underneath. And he didn't shave today, so the light stubble along his chiseled jaw, well it's just plain unfair.

I do my best to ignore the charge between us, that invisible magnetic pull emitting from his large body, still too close to mine, and watch as Dane and Skylar dance to "I Loved Her First." Naturally, a few tears slip out, but I hold up a hand to stop Zach when he tries to sneak closer and comfort me. And then when Whitley and Judd take their mother/son turn to "Simple Man," the tears kick up a notch.

Not only because it's beautiful, and couldn't be a more fitting song for Judd, but it makes me think too hard about another simple man I know, absolutely glorious in his simplicity.

If it's broken, he'll fix it.

You need it? He'll get it.

You want it? He'll find it.

You say it? He'll listen.

That simple.

And when the music starts to play again for everyone to take the floor, JT is right at my side before Zach can do a thing about it, asking me to dance. I jump, literally, at the chance... needing more time to slow down my heart so my head can do the thinking.

I dance with JT, watching Zach watch me with a predatory smolder in his green eyes, as he sways with Emmett. Why Emmett? That'd be because Sawyer won't *stop* dancing with Presley, every song, lest that'd give Blaze an opening to move in.

And in the far corner of the dance floor, seemingly in their own bubble, Brynn is spreading her lil' baby wings... in the arms of Ryder. I've got high hopes for that pairing. Ryder seems like a very nice young man and is obviously enamored by Brynn. Which tells me he's smart too; good eye on him, because she is indeed something special.

So basically, besides Blaze and Presley, just about the only two people who *haven't* danced together at some point tonight are Zach and I. Oh, we've been dancing alright, just *around* it. Us.

"Okay B, we're about to do our thing. Make sure you video it for YouTube." JT ~~tells~~ warns me as the current song comes to an end.

"What exactly are we talking about?" I ask, already frightened of the answer.

"*Pure magic.*" He does some weird jazzy thing with his hands, which I'm really hoping he doesn't replicate in whatever it is he's got planned. "Just get your phone ready!"

I catch on pretty quick what's going on when Whitley plops Skylar down in a chair at the edge of the dance floor and Judd, JT, Ryder and even Blaze, gather together off to the side and all put on sunglasses.

If they're about to do what I think they are, either Blaze is a really fast learner… or wasn't quite the "surprise" arrival he was made out to be. Which, now that I think about it, the guy/girl count in the procession party would've been off had he not *conveniently* shown up. Oh, Miss Presley's gonna hear it from me later about fibbing to her Aunt Bennett. *Busted, princess!*

And here we go. "Lose My Mind" by Brett Eldredge starts playing and the boys take the floor. Whoops and hollers crash through the crowd, hands clapping to the beat. Judd's up front of course, shaking it like a country boy who just got hitched to the girl of his dreams. Skylar's eating it up, laughing through happy tears, as her new husband sings to her about being crazy over her.

Okay, so maybe Blaze really did have to learn the routine on the fly. That or he simply doesn't have even a modicum of rhythm in his entire body. But Ryder's got some pretty good moves, and I glance over; yep, Brynny appreciates them.

The whole thing is precious and I catch all of it on video, slipping in a few JT cameos, because yes, he will run over to watch it, specifically for those.

When all the commotion of the latest surprise has died down, a flash of heat moves over my body and I know, without turning around… Zach Reece is standing right behind me. And he's run out of patience.

Chapter 22

I'm The Man

Zach

Yeah, I'm standing right behind you. And you know it. That's why your flawless skin is in full, rosy bloom and I heard the breathy whimper that just escaped to spite you.

Turn around Bennett. Turn around and let's face this thing head on, together.

I will it, wanting it to happen more than anything I've ever wanted before, but her stubborn lil' ass refuses.

Sure, I could just grab hold and spin her around, take her mouth like I own it, recite back everything she didn't think she was telling me in the hallway last night. But I'm not gonna do it.

Monumental moments call for bold, reckless catalysts. Grandparents don't sit around on their porches and tell the boring stories. No, they tell the ones of life-altering wrinkles in time, tales where words like *"just knew,* BAM, shocking, and overwhelmed" are used, hands are waving around and the enormity of the story shines through their eyes.

I'm Zach fuckin' Reece. I can do spectacular all day long.

And not only do I deserve for *her* to come to *me*… I deserve a story of my own to tell one day.

I walk away the same way I came and can feel her eyes on me with every retreating step.

"Yo!" I catch the DJ's attention, swigging down the last of my drink and handing it to a passing waiter. When the DJ bends to hear me, I tell him my plan. He laughs, but agrees to help me out.

"Good luck." He gives me a fist bump.

Whitley comes flitting across the tent, shoving through the crowd, worrying enough for both of us. "*What* are you doing?" She asks amidst a tight, nervous smile.

"I'm calling her bluff." I state simply.

"You're what?" Her brows pinch, but it's short-lived. Oh." Her mouth makes an "O" and her eyes double in size as realization dawns. "Okay then, go get 'er big boy."

The music stops, Whitley backs away and the DJ taps me on the shoulder with the mic. The air crackles with an electricity of expectancy, so intense I can't possibly be the only one alive with the charge.

Showtime.

"I guess it'd be rude to hijack the spotlight at a wedding without saying something to the lucky couple of honor." I run a hand through my hair. "Skylar, Judd, I love you both very much, and I couldn't be happier for you. In fact, the two of you together, it's been in the making for years." I give a quick, sidelong glance to Bennett, and find her eyes already on mine. "Much like some other things." Her cheeks flame and her eyes drop.

I continue, ignoring the torturous longing in my chest, "I'm proud of you guys for embracing it, despite any obstacles or skepticism you faced in the beginning. For fighting for what you knew you wanted, no matter what anyone else thought. What you knew was right, perfect, inescapable. It's not always easy to take risks, make the first move or put yourself out there, on the chance you may very well just get left hanging." I clear my throat and my head of the thoughts of what that would do to me. "But you kids have inspired me, to say it, once and for all, out loud. And I can only pray I'm not left hanging."

My eyes drift her way, raking over that beautiful, tiny body slowly, heatedly, so she'll feel their touch caress her. "Listen up Bennett Rose Cole, cause I'm talking to you, asking you to tell me if I'm right or if I'm crazy. And it's the last time I'll ask." The room explodes with gasps, whispers and a distinct shout of "bout' damn time!" thrown out by Sawyer... who else?

'You're in so much trouble,' she mouths to me across the dimly lit tent, slicing a finger across her throat.

My lips turn up in a devious smirk. "I sure hope so," I mouth back and set down the mic. To wait.

The music I chose starts and she giggles, shaking her head. She recognizes it instantly: "I'm The Man" by Aloe Blacc.

I lift my brow, the significant question ready for an answer. *Am I the man, Bennett? Your man? Are you gonna tell everybody? Right here, right now—your call gorgeous—shout it from the rooftops or leave me hanging. What's it gonna be?*

I study her, watching the cogs turning in her head from here. The entire Crew sits around her, looking on with what appears to be the same edge-of-your-seat anticipation that's stirring around inside me. And then I see it, the moment when she decides.

To jump.

Literally.

She flies across the floor, pink cheeks wet with tears and leaps into my arms, knowing I'll catch her. Which I do, under the thighs that wrap around my waist as quickly as her arms do around my neck.

"Yes," she rasps solemnly, eyes set on mine. The cheers in the room fade from my ears, my focus solely on her, us.

"Yes what, B?" I need to hear it.

"Yes, you are the man. *My* man." Her tears smother her long-awaited, sweetly spoken promise.

"You're god damn right I am." I rumble, and unapologetically, carry her out of that tent as fast as my feet will move.

There's clapping in the distance as well as multiple shouts of encouragement that I could give two fucks to interpret or acknowledge. I finally have the only thing I want.

But Sawyer, well, when he wants to be heard… he gets heard. "Don't mind us Zennett, ya'll go do your thing, I'll hold down the wedding!"

Zennett… wherever Presley is, she's giggling right now, guaranteed; scary how alike her and her Dad's minds work.

"Where are we going?" She asks against my skin, placing hungry, open-mouthed kisses on the strained column of my neck, making my head spin.

Hell if I know, but I can assure you, it's not all the way up to either one of our suites. I've been waiting to be back inside Bennett for so damn long, I'm half delirious at merely the thought of finding my way back there.

We crossed over from anticipation to excruciation a long, long time ago.

"Bennett, I can't wait. Gotta have you now, baby." My voice is thick and unsteady, much like my cock.

"Yes." She stops sucking on my neck and looks around frantically. "There." She points to a small, striped tent. "It's one of the catering stations. *Hurry*," she whines, adorably, gripping my sides tighter with her thighs, rubbing her core against the hard-on in my shorts.

"Out, now!" I roar at the poor woman cleaning up inside the tent. She drops a plate and runs out, cussing me under her breath. If she only knew, she'd forgive me, I'm sure of it.

I brace Bennett's perfect ass on one arm and use the other to clear everything off the table with one, big sweep. Shit flies everywhere, crashes to the ground… ask me if I give a single, solitary damn.

The second I sit her down on the end of the table, chaos immediately ensues. There's nothing even remotely sophisticated or savvy about it, no coordination whatsoever to our total devouring of each other. Mouths gnash almost painfully together and hands explore hectically as we meld into one. She hisses in my mouth and traps my bottom lip between her teeth as I tug my hands through her hair, tilting her head to kiss her deeper, harder, starvation controlling every frenzied movement. She tastes of champagne and Bennett, her tongue twining with mine, weaving a spell I never want to wake from.

She deprives me of her mouth, ripping open my shirt then grappling frantically with my shorts. "No fucking way," I grunt, snaring both her wrists and pushing her flat onto her back. She *thinks* she wants to fight me, argue, but her jagged breathing won't allow for a lot of talking... and the fiery desire in her eyes is more ravenous than defiant.

I shove both sides of her dress up past her waist, my gaze riveted to the tiny scrap of white lace barely covering my prize. I gradually peel those little panties down her trembling legs and off. I clasp my fingers around her ankles, lifting her feet to rest on the end of the table, then push on the insides of her thighs to spread those sweet legs apart. "Nobody else since, huh?"

I want to hear it again. I want to hear her tell me to my face that no other man's touched this pretty pussy since me.

She blushes and shakes her head no, the fan of her red hair splayed out and swishing across the tabletop with her answer.

"Tell me Bennett. I wanna hear you say it, knowing I can hear you. Tell me who the last man here was."

"Y-you," she pants.

A feral rumble of possession crashes up my chest. "Look at me." Her eyes, a dark, forest green of lust, flicker to mine. "And who will be the last man to ever be here?"

"You." This time there's no stutter, only a solid, reverent pledge.

I touch her, a light finger gliding through her slickness. She's swollen, puffy with want, need, and I can't hold out any longer. I drag her to the very edge of the table and drop to my knees. "You understand," I blow hot breath on her, "that *you*, this pussy, every part of you, are mine now, forever. From here out, no more games, Bennett. You with me?"

"Yes, God, yes Zach. *Please.*"

"Just making sure." I chuckle, my soul as at peace as it's ever been. *She's with me.* I take in the heady scent of her want and lower my head to cover her sweet, glistening cunt with my mouth. Damn but that first taste—*unreal.* The one time before, I didn't eat her. If I had, I'd had pushed her a lot sooner and harder than I did, cause I'm never going without this again.

I have to hold her hips down to keep her from writhing right off the table. "You like that, baby?"

"Mhmmm," she hums, shifting her hips up, begging for my mouth to return.

I dive back in all too willingly, licking up her essence, getting off on the sexy noises she makes, the way she digs her fingers into my forearms.

"More, Zach. So close." Her voice tremors, like her thighs.

I drive two fingers inside her and she winces just a bit. It's a snug damn fit, and my cock twitches, wanting to feel that tightness for himself. I work her slowly, stretching her, just savoring the silken feel of her and the fact we're once again, finally, acknowledging the undeniable connection between us. I stroke her until I hit the spot that has her thrusting herself faster against my hand and purring like a kitten.

"You wanna come just like this baby, or you want my mouth too?"

"Yes!"

My lip quirks up at her delirious non-reply. Guess I'll decide for her, and my decision is "yes" to everything, dipping my head for more. To join my fingers.

I twirl my tongue around her clit, faster then slower, never stopping my fingers from rubbing the glory spot deep inside her. When her inner muscles are twitching and she's chanting my name breathlessly, I grip on to the pulsing little nub with my teeth and hold it firm, flicking my tongue against it rapidly and press down harder with my fingers.

"Oh, *fuck*." It's one long wail, her head thrashing from side to side as she explodes in my mouth, coating my fingers and tongue with her silky, wet warmth.

My lil' tiger, her blood boiling as red-hot as her hair and kiss-swollen lips, doesn't stop and rest for a second, like most women would, sated and wanting to rest in the afterglow of her orgasm. No, *my girl* springs up off her back and pounces, attacking my mouth, neck, ear.

God help me, the ear. Or rather, what she begs, richly delicate in it. "Fuck me, Zach. Fuck me now."

Our hands scramble together to get my shorts and boxer briefs off.

Bennett's a very petite girl; thus the years of dancing standing on my feet, the rides at the fair we've never be able to ride together and the fact that all the top cabinets at her house are empty. And yet, there's never seemed to be more of her than there does right now I want to feast between her legs forever. I want to lick every last inch of her skin. I never want to stop kissing her mouth and my hands itch to trace and memorize every part of her.

But she wants to be fucked.

And yeah, that's definitely on my list too.

We can go slow next time.

I grip the base of my achingly hard cock and line up with her dripping wet center, easing in deliberately, eyes glued to where we join. "Mhmm, Zach," she moans for me and I glance up, needing more than anything to see the look on her face as I enter her. Tears swim in her eyes and I freeze.

"Am I hurting you?"

"No," she laughs faintly, which does insane things with her muscles currently encasing the head of my dick. "Actually, I finally *don't* hurt anymore."

My sweet girl. "I don't either, baby. I don't either." I lean over her to kiss her lips, bracing my weight on my forearms bracketed on either side of her head, and infuse in the kiss my understanding of what we really just said to one another. No more pain, emptiness, longing that never comes to fruition. The wondering and insecurity can't hurt us anymore; we're together now.

Mouths melded, our tongues mingle and twist in cadence to my glides in and out of her. Nothing has ever felt more natural, more in sync. Her velvet to my steel, her tiny, soft body pliant and giving underneath my hard, big one.

She pulls up her feet and digs her heels into my ass, spurring me to go deeper, or faster, or both. "Make love to me later, all night. But right now, right now you fuck me hard Zachary Reece. I need it."

I tried to control myself, take great care with her fragile, unpracticed body, but when the love of your life tells you to fuck her... you fuck her.

I interlace our hands by her head and lay farther over her, driving into her now like a rutting animal, primitive and uncontrollable. She matches my passion, constricting around me in a way that has me clinging to my endurance. She's so skintight that there's not one part of my dick not being cushioned and stroked by her. The exotic mixture of lilac, sweat and mind-blowing sex surrounds us and the little mewls and whimpers coming from her as I slide out to the tip then plunge back through her satiny walls with the force she pleaded for completely incinerates my fortitude.

I find her clit and tease mercilessly with my thumb, sucking on her tongue, making sure to hit her g-spot with every drive. "Ben, baby, come *for* me, with me. You close?"

Her answer is a loud shrill, that they *may* have heard over in the wedding tent, along with her full-body quake. I let my head fall back as I tumble over with her, a roar tearing from my throat as I empty years of denied hunger inside her.

Chapter 23

Up You Go

Bennett

"You cannot be serious." I laugh, trying to squirm away. Not an easy feat when you're pinned under the massive, glorious body of one Zachary Taylor Reece.

"Do I *feel* serious?" He says despite a mouthful of my breast, his still hard cock sliding suggestively against my pussy.

After what I'm hoping was a discreet escape from the catering tent, we'd come back here to his suite and loved each other again. But the second time, we'd taken *our time*, somewhat controlling ourselves and slowing down long enough for both of us to get completely naked so we were free to explore every single part of the other.

He'd made love to me. Unhurried and methodical. Skimming his fingertips along my skin, licking and kissing a path down, then back up my body as he paid me and my body praise in a rich, deep reverence. And... spent *a lot* of time making sure my boobs didn't feel left out. In fact, he's still hanging out there now; he seems to *really* like them.

"Zach." I push on his head, trying to get him to detach from my nipple long enough to look at me, but he refuses to budge or be sidetracked. "As excited as *my girl* is you're back, and very, very good to her, I'd like to be able to walk tomorrow. No sense in wearing out your shiny new toy all in one night."

He is literally in the midst of a just-the-tip moment down there, I guess thinking I won't notice.

I noticed.

"*Ben.*" I'd say he whines it, but the throaty way he turns my name into a plea is way too sexy to ever be called a whine. "Give me some choices, a compromise." Look at him, so objective... while poking the tip in and out.

"You're insatiable." I snicker, pushing on him again. "How about this? Let me take a bath, soak *things* and while I do that, you order us some replenishments. Carbs, definitely carbs, and then we'll see what happens."

He pouts, hottest damn thing I've ever seen, because it's not like a pooched out lip, bratty tantrum kind of thing, but more so a man on fire who's about to combust because he wants you so badly telling you so with his frown. But, reluctantly, he agrees, giving me one more kiss that almost has me changing my mind, then climbs off me. "You want me to run to your room and get any of your girly bath stuff?" He asks.

God he's magnificent, just standing there, comfortable in all his naked glory—with good reason. His hair's skewed from my greedy hands and his sea-green eyes are sparkling. This trip has added a golden glow to his skin, stretched tight over sinewy muscles. Those broad shoulders, decorated with bold, dark ink, a trim waist and defined abs. Yeah, Zach's a looker, no denying it.

And his hands rest on his hips, which are connected to the ridges that cut perfectly down to his dick, as big and beautiful as the rest of him.

"You rethinking that bath?" His flirty tone interrupts my perusal and I force myself to drag my eyes away from his physique to his face, where a smug smirk waits for me. "I love it when you look at me like that, Ben. Trust me, the feeling's mutual."

How did I resist him for so long?

"N-no." I lick my parched lips. "I need a hot bath. And yes, I'd love my stuff, if you really don't mind running to get it?"

"Don't mind at all, baby." He starts to get dressed, and I dash for the bathroom, before I'm tempted again to change my mind. "Be right back," I hear him call over the water I've started running in the tub.

As soon as there's enough ran to sit in, I do so, easing myself down into the warm relief. Not gonna lie, I'm more than a little sore. It's sort of like… say you were once a rock climber and for some reason you suddenly quit doing it, for *years and years*, then one day just decided to run out and scale Mt. Everest—without any warm-up climbs or stretching.

Feels a lot like that.

Not that I'm complaining.

Moreover, as I lower myself farther into the water, lying my head back to rest on the ledge and close my eyes, I have to wonder.

How am I so blessed? What did I ever do to warrant such favor from Heaven? You always hear people say, "God makes one special someone for everyone." Well, he made two for me. He sent Tate into my life, or rather he sent me hall crawling into his room, and I was loved, well and truly. And I returned that love, completely. But then, when God obviously had another plan, one I thought would completely break me, shattering me into so many pieces I'd never be put back together… turns out, he didn't forget about me at all. No, he just changed the plan… and sent me Zach.

And once again, I find myself well and truly loved. And I return it, have for years, completely.

God must really like redheads.

Or maybe he simply likes me. And wants me to be happy. And what kind of person would I be if I didn't take that gift and pay it forward?

A shitty one.

Therefore, I'm gonna make Zach so damn happy, he won't know what hit him.

"Ben!" I startle when he yells and jolt upright. "Damn baby, I just got you, so no drowning yourself in the bathtub please." His laugh is facetious, worry lines on his forehead and around his eyes evident.

I guess I'd fallen asleep while the water was still running. Surely it would've woken me up when it got to my face, but once again… Zach's right there when I need him.

"Okay sleepyhead, you ready to get out? Think we should get you to bed." He doesn't wait for my decision, pulling out the drain plug. "Up you go." He lifts me from the tub and sets me on my feet. Grabbing only one towel for me, oblivious to the fact his own clothes are now soaked, he lets his eyes roam leisurely over my wet, naked body once then shakes his head as though clearing it from a fog. His voice is gravelly when he tells me, "I grabbed your shorts thing you like to sleep in too." He points to the outfit on the counter as he dries me off, quite meticulously I might add, leaving no spot untouched.

"But I promised—"

"Shh." He chastely kisses me quiet. "You didn't *promise* anything. You said we'd see what happens. I saw. You fell asleep in the bathtub. Time for bed, gorgeous."

Another thing "they" say, and it's absolutely true: you don't realize a good thing until it's gone.

But when it, or something just as wonderful, comes back... that's a real eye-opener!

I stand there, like a limp, sleepy rag doll as Zach takes care of me. Drying me off, helping me into my pajamas, even running a brush through my damp hair. We brush our teeth side by side, then he's hoisting me up in his arms once more. "Up you go." He smiles, kissing the end of my nose and carrying me to the bed.

He strips out of his wet clothes, back down to only his navy boxer briefs and climbs in beside me, tucking me into his side and pulling the covers over us. I drape one arm across his stomach and rest my head in the crook of his arm. "You set an alarm?" I ask.

"For what?"

"We fly home tomorrow. We'll need to get up early to pack and stuff." I sigh softly, a bit glum that it's over. "You know it's funny, seems like we were here forever, *waiting* for the wedding. But the minute it's over, we're leaving as fast as we can. Now that

I'm officially exhausted, the work's all done and I need a vacation, the vacation's over."

"Doesn't have to be," he says matter-of-factly, chin resting on top of my head.

"What do you mean?"

"Let's stay for a while, just me and you, alone."

And he's right, we *would* be alone. Sky and Judd aren't even honeymooning here. I mean, why would they want to honeymoon in Jamaica, right? No... they're going straight from this island paradise to, wait for it, Montana. See, married five minutes and they're already compromising. She got to pick the beach wedding, he got to pick the wilderness honeymoon.

"What about work, stuff at home?" I ask.

His body shakes with his soft laughter. "Ben, the gym will run without you for a while, it's why you pay a manager. And I don't teach or coach when school's not in session. And I guess you'll have to fill me in on what this "stuff" at home is you're talking about, cause, far as I can remember, neither one of us owns a pet."

Oh, my God, he's right. We have absolutely nothing stopping us. Suddenly, I don't feel quite so sorry for myself that I'm old, or without young kids.

We could lounge around the beach, rubbing lotion on one another's bodies, make love in the sand at dusk, order room service and eat it off each other. Hang the "Do Not Disturb" sign and sleep in as late...

And just when I had it all envisioned and was excited to agree to stay... jealousy rears her ugly head, fangs and claws bared.

"Or we could go somewhere else," I start with a casual lilt, but end in a catty snarl, "where *Tia* doesn't work."

"Anywhere you want, baby." He chuckles. "Name it. And who's Tia?"

"Who's Tia he says," I grumble, poking him in the ribs. "Seriously though, you really wanna just pick somewhere and go, just like that?"

"I really do. Look at me, Ben." I lift my head. He's grinning down at me, the carefree mirth in his eyes stifling. "I love you, Bennett. I've been so in love with you for too long to remember and I'll be in love with you every day for the rest of my life. If you ask me to, I'll follow you anywhere. And if you ask me to lead, I'll do that too, baby. Just say the word. Oh, and say you love me too." He smirks.

I crawl over him and lay on top of his body, my ear directly over his thrumming heartbeat. "I love you too, Zach. I'm sorry it took me so long to say it. To realize. Thank you for waiting."

He rubs my back. "Totally worth the wait."

"Liar." I snicker. "It was torture and you know it. For me too. When I'm able to keep up with these sexathons you're planning, *then*, you can say it was *totally* worth it."

"So much more than that, Ben. You already know that though."

I do know, but much like my body, my openness with profound statements of feelings will take some building up too.

"So," I quickly change the subject, "where should we go? You lead."

"Well…" He goes silent for a moment, I assume to ponder. "I have an idea, but you're gonna think I'm being corny."

"Guys always think "sweet" means "corny." It doesn't. Sweet is nice, and far too rare. Let's hear it."

"I remember this young girl." He wraps both arms around me tight and whispers on my hair where his lips rest, "that was so excited when she got the lead in "A Street Car Named Desire.""

My eyes well up with tears and my heartbeat speeds up to an excited stammer. *He remembers.*

"She practiced and practiced, talked about it non-stop. She would've blown the audience away, but she never got the chance to take the stage because, like I'd soon come to learn more and more, she always puts others ahead of herself. Do you happen to know what city is depicted in that classic?"

I harrumph, albeit playfully. "Of course I know. *Do you?*"

"I do. You ever been?"

"No," I utter, too overcome with emotion to speak clearly.

"New Orleans it is then, baby."

I lunge forward and latch onto his mouth, borrowing his breath because he just took mine away.

Suddenly, too excited and deeply moved to possibly sleep, I slip off my bottoms, pull his down and raise up atop him, lifting my hips and guiding him inside me. As I lower myself down onto his steel length leisurely, absorbing the feel of every inch, I tell him in a breathy, lust-laden voice, "Don't ever stop doing sweet."

Epilogue

Laney Jo Kendrick

When the DJ announces this will be the last song of the night, a bizarre combination of feelings wash over me and I freeze. On one hand, I'm relieved it's over and my daughter got her dream wedding. But on the other hand, I can't help but feel an immediate void, the sudden open spot in the nest leaving a hollow pull in my stomach; Skylar is married.

A million scattered thoughts, thanks and memories flash through my mind and finally make sense, meshing together into one big picture: happy.

Content, I bring myself back to the present and my eyes naturally seek out Dane. He's already looking at me, much like I often turn to find him doing, and my serenity strengthens. He winks at me and mouths "it's all okay, baby," then begins dancing with my mom.

My dad, her "Pops," grabs his Brynny to end the night dancing with his baby grandchild.

I spot JT, my only son and total Mama's boy, dancing with Macie, and smile, glad they're where I can see them and not off doing things I do not want to know about together.

And then... I find myself searching out the one person I really should share this song with— "Same Old Lang Syne" By Dan Fogelberg. *God, what a great song.*

It's as if the fates planned it, because just as my eyes land on him, he's already walking toward me.

"May I have this dance, Laney Jo?" Evan asks, bright blue eyes holding a tiny fear, as if he thinks for one second I might say no.

"It'd be my pleasure." I smile and move into his arms. I try not to think about the words to the song, heart-wrenchingly appropriate, or I know I'll start crying. Not necessarily sad tears, just those of reminiscence; where we started and all the love, hurt, growing pains and lessons it took to get where we are now. Dancing like two old friends.

He must read my mind, or my expression. "I know." He smiles, that same boyish one full of charm that he's always had, leaning in to kiss my cheek. "I know."

I chance a glimpse at Dane and shockingly, he grins at me and nods... in understanding.

I focus back on Evan. "Who'd have thought? My daughter and your son." I shake my head. "Funny how things work out, isn't it?"

"Can't say that same thought hasn't crossed my mind a time or two." He laughs, again, the same one he's had since the day he came crashing in on my fishin' trip. "And for a long time I felt guilty, because every once in a while, I'd catch myself wondering... where we went wrong." He twirls me out and back in, I know to stall and find some strength to inject in his voice. "Then I'd see the way you look at Dane; the very same way I look at Whitley, and started thinking instead about what went right. Best I can figure, that's what was missing, those two. 'Cause when you and me added in some Dane and Whitley, look what we got: Skylar and Judd. And that... is perfection."

I swallow my sob but don't manage to catch the tear. He does, with his thumb. "Don't cry, Laneybug. It all worked out exactly how it was supposed to. And now, I get to watch you and Whit fight over grandkids." This laugh is real, and I join him. "T-ball or pageants. Oughta be interesting."

"Yeah." I sigh, watching my beautiful daughter Sky dance with her new husband Judd, the perfect young man who reminds me so much of his father it's uncanny. "Look at them." I nudge my head their direction. "They do look pretty darn perfect. Heck, look at all of us." I say, meeting Evan's eyes once again. "I'd say we did good, Tod."

"We sure did, Copper. We sure did."

Acknowledgements

First and foremost, I want to thank those who have endured it all with me, the good and bad, without fail: my wonderful husband Jeff, without whom I would literally lie down and give up; my patient, understanding daughters, who support me by accepting me as is; and my family. I'm so thankful for all of you and love you more than anything in the whole world.

Angela Graham, my best friend and CP, I couldn't do it without you, girl. Every hurdle we ALWAYS jump only makes our asses and thighs look better! So, here's to the strength of "us." From day one to the end, you and me. Me and you. I love you very much.

Jill Sava, you're so damn amazing, a true inspiration! Thank you for knowing when to just ignore how I said to do it and do it the right way. Thank you for being so level-headed and focused on the things that matter. I'd be lost without you, and I love you!

My bangin' betas: Jill Sava, Ashley Jasper, Linda Cotter, Amber Warne, Alison Evans-Maxwell, Kara Hildebrand, and Angela Doughty, thank you so much ladies for lovin' the Crew and helping me make Endure the best it could be! I appreciate you all so much!

Elite, you're the best group of women I've ever met all in one place, and that shit usually does not work out, lol… too many women in a group? No, just no. But you guys, well, you're ELITE. Loving, empathetic, kind, caring, and full of true character. I adore and appreciate every single one of you!

Crew, YOU LADIES ROCK!!!! Thank you for all the fun, love and support!!!!! I'm so lucky to have you!

Hilary Storm, because it's real; you, me, you and me. I'm blessed by our friendship, and thank you for it!

Erin Noelle, forever and always, Smoops. Love you. xoxox

Jessica Prince, good lookin' out, Boo! THANK YOU for that idea jamfest!!!!

Monique Hite- I thought about writing out everything you mean to me, and then it hit me… I only have to say one thing and she'll know exactly what all those few words say to her, thank her for. **ROD, Moe. ROD.**

Sommer Stein, as always, sis… you amaze me, support me, and make it so easy! I'm so grateful for you and your magic! Xo

Shelby Leah, you pretty girl, thank you so much for my beautiful cover!!!! Love you! xoxoxo

Brenda Wright- Could I BE a bigger pain in your ass? I hope you still love me though, cause I damn sure love the hell out of you!

Kay Springsteen, thank you so much for your friendliness, eye for detail and willingness to put up my disorganized, panicky butt! I appreciate it! xo

Tabby Coots, Kimberly Reynolds and Rachelle Jones, for your fast fingers and willingness to always help me out! Without the three of you, my books would be written in Sharpie on paper and never typed. I can't tell you how much I appreciate your help! XOXO

And to all the readers and bloggers who support me and my books, making it possible for me to do what I love for a living, my endless, undying appreciation and thanks! You're all amazing!

If I forgot you, not only am I sorry, but feel free to come give me the ass kickin' I'm sure I'm long overdue for!

About the Author

S.E.Hall, lover of all things anticipation and romance, is the author of The Evolve Series: Emerge, Embrace, Entangled, Entice and Baby Mama Drama, as well as the stand-alone novel Pretty Instinct. Her co-written works included The Provocative Professions Collection: Stirred Up, Packaged and Handled, One Naughty Night and full-length novel Matched with Angela Graham as well as Conspire, a romantic suspense with Erin Noelle.

S.E. resides in Arkansas with her husband of 18 years and 3 daughters of the home. When not writing or reading, she can be found "enthusiastically cheering" on one of her girls' softball games.

S.E. Hall

Newsletter: http://eepurl.com/7E-nP

Facebook: https://www.facebook.com/S.E.HallAuthorEmerge

Amazon: http://www.amazon.com/S.E.-Hall/e/B00D0AB9TI/

Twitter: https://twitter.com/Emergeauthor

Tumblr: http://sehallauthor.tumblr.com/

Other Books by
S.E. Hall

FINALLY FOUND NOVELS

Pretty Instinct

Pretty Remedy

CO-WRITTEN BESTSELLERS

WITH ANGELA GRAHAM

Matched

Stirred Up

Packaged

Handled

Handled 2

One Naughty Night

WITH ERIN NOELLE

Conspire